YOURDRUM

Kevin Stock

SCRIPTIS

YOURDRUM

By KEVIN STOCK

ISBN 978-0-99679-890-7 (paperback)

ISBN 978-0-9967989-2-1 (hardback)

ISBN 978-0-9967989-1-4 (EPub)

Library of Congress Control Number: 2015951692

Library of Congress subject headings:

1. Fiction / Visionary & Metaphysical
2. Fiction / Science Fiction / General
3. Fiction / Literary

2016

Published by:

 SCRIPTIS

Scriptis LLC

12852A Town and Four

St. Louis, MO 63141

www.yourdrum.org

Dedicated to:

This story is dedicated to the dreamers.

This is for the believers.

This is for the difference makers who dare to cause a raucous and challenge the status quo.

This is for the outliers who risk imagining, exploring, and creating.

This is for the bold, the inventors, the achievers; those who pick themselves.

This is for the unconventional, the non-conformists; those courageous enough to stand on the other side of the majority.

This is for the remarkable.

This is for you, the engine, the power, the force that carries the world forward.

This is for you who are unapologetically — You.

TRAVELS OF YOURDRUM

"the story in the book can create the story of the book"

Name: Kevin

From (where you purchased/received/found it):

Original copy

Passed Along (where you gifted/dropped/sent it):

To Meng:
A guiding light and epitome
of yourdrum.

Name: Alison

From (where you purchased/received/found it):

Mailbox

Passed Along (where you gifted/dropped/sent it):

Car window (⁀‿⁀)

TRAVELS OF YOURDRUM

"books that are loved are let go"

Name: _____

From (where you purchased/received/found it):

_____

_____

Passed Along (where you gifted/dropped/sent it):

_____

_____

_____

Name: _____

From (where you purchased/received/found it):

_____

_____

Passed Along (where you gifted/dropped/sent it):

_____

_____

_____

Travels of Yourdrum

"a good book has several stories"

Name: _____

From (where you purchased/received/found it):

_____

_____

Passed Along (where you gifted/dropped/sent it):

_____

_____

_____

Name: _____

From (where you purchased/received/found it):

_____

_____

Passed Along (where you gifted/dropped/sent it):

_____

_____

_____

TRAVELS OF YOURDRUM

"some books float on the surface, some sink deeper"

Name: _____

From (where you purchased/received/found it):

_____

_____

Passed Along (where you gifted/dropped/sent it):

_____

_____

_____

Name: _____

From (where you purchased/received/found it):

_____

_____

Passed Along (where you gifted/dropped/sent it):

_____

_____

_____

Travels of Yourdrum - Continued in back of book

Contents

PART I:

Dreams

"Maybe the world was right," he thought to himself. *"Maybe it was a mistake."*

Six months ago the young doctor closed his practice. He believed he had uncovered the secret; the answer to the epidemic; and he was risking everything to focus on developing a device to help people sleep. Joseph had only been a doctor for just over year. In the solitude of his lab, he wondered if the naysayers were right.

"Who was he to invent something?"

"What did he know?"

"Who did he think he was?"

These were the questions Joseph was sure his friends, family, and colleagues were asking behind his back.

His parents feared he had thrown it all away. They wondered why he couldn't be more level-headed like his three brothers.

Joseph's older brother was an established, highly-respected, and regarded surgeon. An influential voice in the medical community, he had the prestige and respect that Joseph only hoped he could achieve someday.

Joseph had two younger brothers, as well.

The youngest was a banker with much promise. Zachary had rapidly moved up the corporate ladder. He knew good deals and wise investments when he saw them. He also had a keen sense when people who needed loans would be unable to repay their debts. His lending prudence seemed harsh to many, but his bosses praised it.

Joseph's other brother was a lawyer who specialized in collecting debts. He and Zachary made a good team.

Everyone around Joseph wondered what was wrong with him. By all accounts, he had made it. He was a doctor; he had esteem, a high income, and a secure future. He had spent his entire life getting to this point. After years of study, struggle, and sacrifice, he had "made it." And he was throwing it all away on some hunch, some idea, some crazy theory he devised.

Sitting with his head in his hands, Joseph couldn't help but think that maybe the naysayers were right; maybe he should forget about this invention, bury the idea, act like it never occurred to him, and see if he could somehow get back to practicing medicine.

Sighing, Joseph raised his head. Sitting by the lone window in his tiny, one-room apartment — his "lab" — he stuck his head out of the window, hoping to catch the breeze. Beads of sweat rolled down his face. The summer heat was relentless, especially since he had turned off the air conditioning the week before. He bet all of his savings on the device's development; what little money he had left needed to go to food, not cool air.

As he wiped a bead of sweat from his forehead, he turned to stare at the periodic table of elements that hung above his "workbench," his simple wooden table that sat in the middle of his apartment.

‡

Before becoming a doctor, Joseph had studied chemistry. This was a recommendation from his parents. At the time, Joseph had no interest in chemistry; and frankly, he found it quite impractical. However, because of the rigor of the chemistry curriculum, it increased his likelihood of being able to become a doctor. So, Joseph didn't fight it. Becoming a doctor sounded like a good idea. Doctors made a good, consistent, and stable income; they were respected among the community and provided a worthy service to their fellow neighbors.

To Joseph, it sounded nice. It sounded like a good career. It sounded like a good life.

So he pushed through chemistry. The periodic table became his constant companion. Joseph worked hard to memorize the elements, their atomic weights, charges, and affinities. He came to see the world through the eyes of elements, atoms, and molecules.

What fascinated Joseph and lightened the burden of his studies was the periodic table. To Joseph, the elements organized on this chart represented the building blocks of life. With knowledge of the periodic table came an understanding of how things were created from their purest forms. During his studies, these building blocks represented an ethereal concept. Now they were frighteningly relevant to his survival.

For the past six months, Joseph had stared at the periodic table for hours. He hoped it would speak to him and tell him the answer to what he had been looking for. The device he had squandered all his money to create needed to be compatible with the body, soft and integrated, and yet also have the functional capacity of mechanical moving parts. Joseph had been looking for a material that could function like a reliable metal, yet was soft like rubber. He was convinced the periodic table held the solution to his dilemma.

Sitting in the windowsill, he found himself once again staring at the periodic table. This time, however, something was different. Joseph couldn't shake a nagging feeling.

"Something is missing here…"

‡

After four grueling years of chemistry study, Joseph was accepted into medical school. He was reluctantly excited. At his medical school orientation, he recalled the dean telling the class, "You've made it. The hard part is over. You've all been accepted, you are here, and in no time you will all be doctors."

The problem was Joseph didn't feel as if he had made it. He felt like he had four more years of punishment ahead of him. Worse, he felt that his last four years of punishment were a waste. He didn't need physical chemistry, organic chemistry, quantitative analysis, or chemical engineering for any of his medical studies. Except for providing some insights into medicine formulations, chemistry was basically useless.

The education system never made sense to Joseph. To him it seemed every class was a stepping-stone to get to some final destination of actual, applicable knowledge. It seemed like the system was designed to weed people out rather than usher them into the life they desired. It seemed backwards. Instead of choosing what one wanted to learn, a student had to do everything possible in the hope of being chosen. Instead of picking, students were trained to be picked. The system rewarded the art of jumping through hoops, adhering to red tape, and following instructions.

Nonetheless, after another four years of little sleep, lots of caffeine, and stress, it was over.

He had made it. Or so everyone said — *again*. He was a doctor.

Strangely, at graduation, Joseph didn't seem to feel like the other newly-minted doctors. They were rejoicing — they had made it.

"Prestige, money, and a life of safety and security were theirs!"

Instead, the two letters before his name — Dr. — made Joseph feel even more restricted. At the time, he wasn't sure why. Little did he know that in less than a year it would become overwhelmingly clear.

‡

Upon graduation, Joseph opened his own practice. It was a bold move for a 26-year-old, brand new doctor. Most doctors flew under the wings of a hospital or a large, healthcare conglomerate. Their schedules, salaries, and scope of practice were set by the organization. To Joseph, there was something about working for a big hospital or a bureaucratic organization that was off-putting. It seemed restrictive. Just like the two letters before his name.

‡

During his first day in his new practice, Joseph caught a glimpse of his future. As he was examining a patient, checking his vitals, and taking a health history, Joseph watched as the patient slowly blinked his eyes. His head drooped then jerked back up suddenly. He was fighting to stay awake. Finally, he slumped forward with his chin resting on his chest.

From the silence emerged booming snores.

Joseph looked at him incredulously as snores shook the walls.

Then there was silence. Thirty seconds passed.

Joseph looked at the clock. Forty-five seconds. One minute. Still silence. Just as Joseph went to shake his patient awake, a frantic gasp erupted from the man, which woke him up. He shook his head and opened his eyes. As he gathered himself, he apologized for drifting off.

Strangely, these mid-appointment naps became commonplace. Joseph wondered if he needed to liven up his appointments to keep his patients from slumbering in mid conversation.

The trend persisted. People were tired. *They were exhausted.*

"What is going on here?" Joseph wondered on a seemingly daily basis.

Due to the preponderance of patients who couldn't keep their eyes open, Joseph changed his exams. He began to ask every patient about their sleep, energy, and vitality.

"Do you need to nap during the day?" Joseph would ask. "Do you feel tired or drift off easily?"

To his surprise, patients admitted that they often found themselves drifting off at inappropriate times, such as at work and in the middle of the afternoon. They often felt exhausted for no good reason; even getting out of bed in the morning was a burdensome and monumental task for many.

"Doctor, I feel like I need to lie down constantly," a patient explained to Joseph one morning as she sat on the exam table. "After being in bed all night, you would think I would want to get up and get going. But after the struggle of getting up, I can't wait to lie down again. I don't have the energy to get up and about."

"When did you start to notice this?" Joseph asked.

"I guess I'm not exactly sure," she continued. "I remember in school it seemed I could burn the candle at both ends. But I was young. Life was a crazy adventure then. Any given day it seemed like anything could happen. I guess being on my toes was the only option.

"After school, in my first job, I still felt good. I was a low-paid actress doing plays here and there. I loved it, though. Being on stage, in front of the lights, entertaining — it was thrilling!" She smiled at the memory, and Joseph noticed energy in her voice for the first time as she thought back to her youth.

"But it was completely unsustainable. A few years later, I got a regular job with normal hours and higher pay. It was probably about a year or so after settling down as a grownup that I started to notice the fatigue."

"Ok," Joseph said while taking notes, "Here are your prescription refills. The pills with the red label should help with your energy and headaches, and the pills with the blue label should help with the depression."

"Got it. Thank you, doctor."

‡

Day after day, Joseph witnessed more tired patients, more depressed patients. When he analyzed his medication inventory, he discovered that pills to help with depression, fatigue, and headaches were the number one sellers.

"Maybe it's certain foods or lack of exercise or...something." Joseph searched his thoughts for answers. He also searched journals, books, and research publications, which all proved to be lacking.

Joseph reached out to colleagues and friends to see if they were encountering the same symptoms among their patients. One after the other told Joseph that it was normal and not to worry about it. Joseph thought they were hid-

ing from liability and responsibility under the large corporate umbrella that employed them. These doctors followed directions, obeyed the rules, and did as they were
instructed. Anything that would change their protocol or
disrupt the status quo was not to be entertained.

Joseph was resilient though. He wasn't going to pawn off
responsibility. He kept pushing for answers.

Joseph reached out to every medical professional he knew.
He even organized a regional gathering to discuss this
strange phenomenon. He rented out a large hall where
all could sit and discuss. On the night of the gathering,
Joseph was alone. No one showed — not even his brother,
the surgeon.

The more he tried to uncover answers, the more ostracized he became among his peers. But Joseph couldn't
just "let it go," as he colleagues advised.

Joseph began to accept that he was on his own with this
one.

"People are tired because they don't get enough sleep," Joseph reasoned. *"But both tired patients and energized patients say they are sleeping fine."*

It didn't add up.

‡

She was bleeding from head to toe. Scraped knees, elbows, forehead.

Rachel's mother had ordered her to stay out of the woods. But Rachel couldn't help herself. The woods called to her. She constantly dreamed about exploring the hills, climbing the trees, and playing in nature on the other side of town.

"You're too young, you're a girl, and the woods are dangerous," her mother lectured in response to her pleas.

But Rachel never was good about following rules that didn't make sense to her. Rachel and her friends took off exploring in the woods just outside of town. They climbed up hills and trees and came upon a fifteen-foot high cliff with a small, shallow stream rushing below. A massive oak tree stood on the edge of the cliff. A perfect vine hung from its branches, obviously designed by God to be swung out over the stream below.

The adventurous spirits of the young girls looked at the vine with pure thrill. There was no need to ask what to do. Rachel grabbed the vine, tugged on it, and then took several steps back. With a running start, Rachel catapulted out over the embankment. She screamed with delight as she soared over the stream below.

As she swung back on the pendulum towards the top of the cliff to safety, the vine tracked right to the trunk of the oak from which it hung. Rachel slammed into the tree trunk, and dangled from the vine above the stream which was flowing fifteen feet below her.

Rachel swayed back and forth over the stream until her friends were able to pull the vine and their friend to safety. Once back on solid footing, Rachel and her friends looked at each other, fell to the ground, and laughed.

It wasn't until Rachel arrived home to the berating of her mother that she even realized she was hurt.

"What did I say?" Her mother scolded. "I told you not to go into those woods. Now let's get you to the doctor."

Rachel's smile and energy was still upon her when she arrived at Dr. Joseph's office.

"Hi, Doctor!" she said to Joseph.

"How are you feeling?" Joseph asked with a tone of concern, as he started patching up the wounds.

"Great! My friends and I just discovered this amazing new vine we can swing from in the woods!"

"And it's the last time you'll be swinging from it," Rachel's mother sternly interjected.

Even with open wounds, Rachel had excitement and energy that Joseph hadn't seen in his office in quite some time. Rachel, ignoring her mother's demand, continued to tell Joseph about the woods and the amazing tree with the perfect vine for swinging.

"I'm glad to see you are ok," Joseph said. And he leaned in close, whispering into her ear, "But next time, swing out at an angle so you miss the tree trunk when you swing back." Joseph smirked, and Rachel smiled back with a nod.

The emergency appointment set Joseph's schedule back. The waiting room was full, but he didn't mind. Rachel's energy and enthusiasm were infectious. He felt good.

"If only more of my patients had the energy of this adventurous girl," Joseph thought as he walked into the next room.

His next patient was a new patient: 52-year-old Tom. He sat on the patient table wearing a fine suit, his shoes shined, and his tie rested in a perfect knot on top of his designer, button-down shirt.

"How you doing, Doc?" Tom exclaimed with a big smile.

"I'm doing great, thank you. How are you?"

"Fabulous!"

"That's great," Joseph said, shocked to see two patients in a row with lots of energy and enthusiasm.

As Joseph proceeded with the exam, he noticed Tom's watch. He couldn't help but think his house cost less than what Tom was wearing on his wrist.

Joseph launched into his standard questions.

"How is your energy during the day?"

"I would say great. I sleep great and had a wild dream last night; let me tell you…"

Joseph's face blanched. He felt as if he had just been struck by a lightning bolt that turned on a bright light-bulb inside his head.

"That's it." Joseph muttered out loud, unintentionally.

"What's it?" Tom dubiously looked at Joseph.

"Sorry," Joseph smiled, "your energy, your dream…it all makes sense."

Joseph paused, gathered himself, and soaked in the moment of revelation with a wry smile in his heart.

"Let me explain," Joseph started. "Tom, I see patients every day who are burdened with fatigue, depression, constant lethargy and headaches. They lack energy and vitality, and the desire and excitement of life. I have been searching for an answer to get to the root of the problem, instead of masking the symptoms with medications. I have been looking for the cause so that we can fix the problem instead of just treating the effects."

Joseph paused and Tom interjected, "So what do you think the root cause is?"

"Dreams." Joseph smiled.

"Dreams?" Tom shot Joseph a curious look.

"Exactly. People aren't dreaming. You see, there are different levels of sleep. One of the deepest levels of sleep is called REM sleep or Rapid Eye Movement sleep. It's the stage of sleep when we dream. The fact that you are dreaming means you are getting deep restful sleep, and that's why you have energy and feel good during the day!"

Joseph was on cloud nine. He deciphered the code. Or so he thought.

"Oh, I always dream!" Tom said, smiling seeing the light in Joseph's eyes.

"And that's why you have the energy and good health that you do." It all made so much sense to Joseph now.

Joseph knew — or at least had a theory — why so many of his patients were tired, exhausted, and depressed. They weren't dreaming. They weren't getting any REM sleep.

Joseph couldn't wait to test this theory. It was simple. He would question his patients to see if they were dreaming or not. If they reported they weren't dreaming, it would mean they weren't getting the deep REM sleep they needed. Dreaming was the key to their energy, vitality, and life. Joseph surmised that patients who dream should have energy and feel good. It was a simple experiment that he could test right away.

Tom put his hand out to shake Joseph's.

"It sounds like you're on to something, Doc. I can't wait to hear the outcome. Keep me posted. Life is too short not to dream!"

Joseph shook hands with Tom, eager to test his theory.

‡

Over the next several days, Joseph asked his patients about their dreams.

With each patient he wrote in his notebook:

> Patient Name:
>
> Dreaming: Yes/No
>
> Energy: Yes/No
>
> Medications for energy, depression, vitality: Yes/No

The notebook proved conclusive.

Patient after patient confirmed his theory. The tired and de-pressed patients, the ones who had no energy and tended to be the sickest, weren't dreaming. The patients who had lots of energy and vitality and tended to be the healthiest were dreaming.

Again, Joseph reached out to colleagues and friends — the ones who would still speak to him.

They shunned his theory.

His last remaining friends began to turn their backs on him.

[YOURDRUM]

Joseph's closest friend in school tried to rationalize with him by explaining that it was natural to get tired as people age. He told Joseph to keep filling prescriptions — the blue- and red-labeled bottles.

In a last desperate attempt, Joseph tried to get through to his older brother, the renowned surgeon.

"Joseph, this is the last time I am going to tell you," his brother lectured, "there is nothing wrong with decreasing energy levels as people get older. You have already made a bad name for yourself in the medical community; try not to make it worse. And, more importantly, you are starting to tarnish my name with your ridiculous off-the-wall obsession. Drop this lunatic theory of yours, or please don't show up at my house again."

Joseph got the point. His theory was not welcome.

‡

A few weeks passed as Joseph dwelled on creating a fix, a solution so people could start dreaming again. He figured that finding the answer was the only way to validate his theory. And he was going to have to go at it alone.

22

One night as Joseph prepared for bed, he paused and looked at his reflection in the mirror.

"Why are people so tired?" Joseph asked aloud. "It's because they aren't dreaming."

"But why aren't people dreaming?" he asked, as he continued the conversation with himself.

"Because they aren't getting REM sleep," came the reply.

"Buy why aren't they getting REM sleep?" Joseph asked, trying to deduce a solution.

That was the question.

Joseph rested his head on his pillow, eyes wide open staring at the ceiling. His mind raced trying to come up with a plausible solution.

"Obviously, people aren't getting REM sleep because the body is resisting this stage of sleep. But, why would the body resist deep, restorative sleep?" Joseph wondered as he drifted off to sleep.

‡

The sand was soft under his feet. He laid back and enjoyed the tide as it rode in and washed over his legs. The sun setting on the horizon, and the cool breeze relaxed Joseph. He breathed deeply. Air effortlessly filled his lungs. He exhaled slowly.

Out of the corner of his eye he saw someone walking along the beach. He had thought he was alone, the only one within miles of this spot. Joseph got to his feet. It appeared to be a woman. Her back was to Joseph. She had long, dark, wavy hair that flowed in the evening breeze. Joseph began to walk towards her. He estimated she was at least fifty yards away. Joseph picked up his pace, trying to close the gap.

He wasn't making any headway. He picked up his pace to a jog.

"Hello!" Joseph shouted. He didn't want to scare her, but his curiosity overtook his precaution.

She didn't turn, her back still facing Joseph. Joseph's jog turned into a run.

He was barely making any headway, even though she appeared to be just strolling along the beach front where the waves crashed into the shore.

Joseph's run turned into a sprint. He was finally starting to close the gap. From behind, she appeared to be as beautiful and radiant as the falling sun on the horizon. Her long, blue dress blew in the wind.

"Hello?" Joseph shouted.

Still no response.

"Surely she can hear me," Joseph thought, as he closed to about twenty-five yards away.

"Hi! Can you hear me?" Joseph tried again, still sprinting at full steam ahead. It made no sense; she seemed to barely be walking, slowly putting one foot in front of the other, while Joseph was getting short of breath from his sheer exertion.

Ten yards. He was getting closer.

"Hello?" he muttered running out of breath.

No response.

Five yards.

"Excuse me…" Joseph struggled to get words out now. The mysterious woman still didn't turn.

One yard. She was nearly within reach. Joseph was at his all-out, max sprint.

He reached out for her arm.

"Hiiiiiiii…" Joseph gasped, barely able to get the word out through his labored breathing.

He lunged — inches from touching the stranger on the beach.

With a gasp, Joseph shot up in his bed. Panting, heart racing, sweat dripping, Joseph struggled to catch his breath. He couldn't believe how real the dream felt. How intensely he wanted to see her face…

Joseph got up and splashed water on his face. He looked at his reflection in the mirror. He shut his eyes thinking back to the dream — the girl on the beach, the intense struggle trying to see her. His eyes popped open.

"Of course!" he almost shouted.

It was obvious now. The answer to his question, "Why weren't people getting REM sleep?" revealed itself in his dream.

"It's harder to breathe in the dream state." Joseph smiled as he started to catch his breathe.

Joseph reasoned the body resisted the dream state — REM sleep — because breathing was more difficult in this stage of sleep. It made sense. Muscles become paralyzed during REM sleep to prevent the body from acting out its dreams. With the muscles in an immobile, relaxed state, the airway becomes narrower, making breathing more difficult.

Joseph's deductive logic was sound. People were tired because they weren't dreaming. They weren't dreaming because the body was resisting this stage of sleep. The body resisted deep stage REM sleep because breathing was more difficult in this level of sleep.

Dreaming can cause the body some discomfort, therefore it avoids it.

The solution, Joseph determined, was to create a device to make it easier to breathe while sleeping. If breathing was easier, the body wouldn't have any problems going into REM sleep. Then people would start dreaming again.

"Why try and figure out things on my own?" Joseph mused. *"Might as well just sleep on them, and let the answer come to me!"*

Joseph shook his head with a smile as he dressed for the day.

‡

For weeks, Joseph was distracted from his patients. He was deep in his head, trying to think through the intricacies of the device.

Joseph obsessively thought about the device. Every evening, Joseph came home and detailed his daily insights on paper. He drew designs and variations on every possible way the device could connect and integrate with the patient and function to improve breathing. The design had to be elegant. It had to be comfortable and biocompatible, but also mechanical and functional.

Joseph ran some numbers.

He calculated the time it would take to build a prototype. He estimated and added up the potential costs for materials and testing.

Then Joseph had a familiar feeling. He felt the restrictions he had felt at graduation. This time it was tangible, though.

To create this device, he was going to have to leave everything he had worked for behind: the "Dr." before his name; his practice and patients; his safe and secure income; his profession; and what little esteem of being a doctor he had left. Joseph thought of all the sacrifices he had made to get to this point, the long journey, the rigorous studies. He felt the strong grip of resistance trying to hold on to what he had worked so hard to become. He felt the tension between this grip wanting to hold on to what was known and the unknown possibilities of letting go.

It was a lot to give up. He wasn't sure if he could break free from it. The grip was tight.

"Could this theory be right and the whole world oblivious to it? Could I really know something and make something that no one else had thought of or done before?"

He was going to sleep on it.

‡

Joseph continued treating patients in his practice. His theory continued to prove itself. Not once had he found a patient who was tired and depressed but still dreamed. The correlation between dreaming and having energy and vitality and not dreaming and being tired and depressed was perfect.

Every night, Joseph ran through options in his head.

Option #1: He could continue in his practice. He would prescribe blue- and red-labeled pills, make a good income, and live securely all the way to death. He would forget about this "dreaming thing" and regain the support and comradery of his family and friends. He would live with the prestige of being a doctor and have the satisfaction of a respectable life.

Option #2: He could attempt to create this device that has only been seen in his imagination and that no one else believes in. He would have to spend all his money, all his time, risk everything…and maybe it would work. Maybe it wouldn't. His family would be upset that he threw everything away, angry for his financial irresponsibility, and worried about his mental health; his friends would scoff at his naivety and stupidity. In the silence of his lonely existence, he would hear the whisperings of others talking of his insanity.

Joseph couldn't help but notice that Option #2 didn't seem too pleasing. Option #1 seemed much more appealing. He couldn't decide. Little did he know, not making a decision was a decision nonetheless.

Joseph's daily routine of seeing patients continued. A month passed.

‡

"AHH!"

Joseph awoke before dawn with a searing headache, a pounding in his head. He sat up, holding his head with both hands, applying heavy pressure to his temples. It was Sunday morning, and he didn't have to be up for hours.

Ba-boom, ba-boom, ba-boom — his head felt like it was literally shaking from the beating. Joseph stumbled out of bed to get dressed. The pounding in his head was so extreme he couldn't bend over to tie his shoes. He had to get to the office.

Fumbling with his key to unlock the office door, he was finally able to match the lock and key and get in. He ripped open his prescription cabinet, grabbed the red-labeled medication, and stuffed a handful of pills down his throat. He lay on an exam table, waiting and praying for the pounding to stop.

After several agonizing minutes, the drug started doing its job. The drumming quieted.

‡

From that day on, Joseph had a new routine. Every morning, he awoke to a drumming in his head. He would proceed to stumble to his medicine cabinet and pull out the red-labeled pills he had prescribed for himself. He would take the pills and lay back down until the drumming had quieted enough to start his day.

After weeks of implementing this new routine, the drumming was finally starting to abate. It was finally getting softer and slower. And so was Joseph.

He didn't see as many patients as he did a few months ago. He stopped asking them about their sleep and dreams. Joseph needed naps in the middle of the day to get him through the afternoon. He couldn't be seen without a cup of coffee in his hand. At home, he found himself snoring on the couch shortly after dinner.

Joseph was glad he had ostracized himself from his friends, family, and peers, as he had no interest or energy for socializing. He was unhappy.

Joseph decided to prescribe himself the blue-labeled pills to accompany his red ones.

‡

One sunny morning, Joseph awoke to the beat of light drumming in his head that he had become accustomed to. Some painkillers and shortly he would be fine.

As Joseph arrived at the office, he was stopped in his tracks. His first patient was already there, beaming.

"Hey, Doc!" It was Tom, his attire as high class as before.

To Joseph, Tom's greeting sounded like a shout; the drumming came back with a vengeance.

"I'm going to need some more painkillers," Joseph thought, as he dragged himself into his office.

"You're early," Joseph remarked.

"Yes, sir! I hate to waste sunshine by sleeping it away. And, I had another wild dream I have to tell you about!" Tom excitedly replied.

It hit Joseph like a hammer.

"Dream? I can't remember the last time I had a dream."

The drumming was at full force.

Tom hopped onto the exam table as he asked, "By the way, how is that sleep experiment going?"

There was something about this man. He exuded energy, enthusiasm, and life. Joseph couldn't lie to him. He desperately wanted to say that his theory was wrong — that he was wrong. He wanted to shove a handful of pain-killers down his throat to silence the beating drum in his head. Tom's presence and questions were dredging up the idea Joseph had abandoned months ago.

"The experiment was pretty, um, conclusive," Joseph honestly and sheepishly replied.

"That's great!" Tom exclaimed. "So have you thought of a solution?"

"Well, I had an idea…" Joseph wasn't sure how Tom was getting this out of him. He hadn't thought of the device in months.

"And?" Tom prodded.

"And, well, I'm not sure it will work."

"Why not?" Tom asked, unrelenting to Joseph's apathy.

"Well, umm, it's never been made before."

"Of course it's never been made before!" Tom bellowed. "If it had been, we wouldn't be having this discussion!"

Tom put his hand on Joseph's shoulder and asked, "Do you think you can make it?"

"I did some calculations awhile back. It would take all my time and the little money I have managed to save."

Ba-boom. Ba-boom. Ba-boom. Joseph squeezed the back of his neck.

"Doc, with all due respect, that's selfish. The world needs this from you. Don't keep it from them."

"It doesn't even exist; how am I keeping it from them?" Joseph responded defensively.

"Have you imagined it? Do you believe you can make it?" Tom persisted.

"I guess so."

"Well, then, it's possible. If you bury it and keep it from the world, you are holding back a gift — selfishly."

Joseph knew he was right. It was clear what he had to do. Tom unburied the device that Joseph had deeply covered with pills and fear disguised as rationalizations. His self-justifications truly were the voice of hell.

"You're right. I'm going to make it."

In that moment, Joseph took a leap. He stared into the face of fear. Instead of retreating, this time he jumped right into it. He committed. He was going to create it.

The drumming that was becoming deafening silenced.

The calm in his head was as refreshing as a still lake at dawn. The fogginess that had bogged him down for weeks cleared, colors brightened, energy returned.

Joseph had his assistant cancel appointments for the rest of the day, the rest of the week, and indefinitely.

He closed his practice that day.

Joseph's practicality was revealed for what it was — fear. Confronting this fear head on, Joseph relinquished the comfort and security of his profession — the "Dr." he had worked his life on attaining — and released the grip that had held on so tightly to the safety of the status quo. He was liberated from the confinement of conforming to the conventional.

He was free.

‡

Joseph spent the next couple weeks getting his affairs in order. He sold his nice home in the upscale suburbs. He sold all his possessions except for the bare essentials. He found his new "lab" — a one-room apartment in the outskirts of the city. It was a cheap apartment, but it backed to a beautiful, small, tree-lined lake. He bought a "workbench," an easel for design work, and materials. He unrolled his massive periodic table that he had stored away years ago. He pinned it up. It completely covered the bare wall. His lab was ready.

The first night in his lab, Joseph sat next to the lone window, watching the sunset and fireflies start to glow. His future had never been so uncertain, yet he had never been so free. It was like the chains and tensions of "normal" life were lifted; and he could go, do, and be as his heart desired. With this freedom came a sense of awe, openness, and infinity. The impossibilities of the sleep device seemed not only possible, but imminent and assured. He felt powerful, with a sense of invincibility. He felt he was in charge of his destiny.

For once, instead of constantly reacting, Joseph had acted.

As he stared out the window, looking over the small lake behind his lab, Joseph saw movement among the shadows. The leaves on the tress that lined the lake rustled. The evening breeze was quiet yet steady. Joseph made out the shadow of a person. It was a woman. She looked familiar. Her dress and hair waved in the wind.

"She looks just like the woman in that dream," Joseph thought.

No sooner than he had the thought, the woman glanced in the direction of Joseph's window. It was her. In that instant, his eyes connected with the most captivating eyes he had ever seen. Her deep, blue eyes contrasted against her long, dark hair. Even in the fading sunlight, he could see how beautiful she was.

As Joseph stared out the window, his attention was diverted by a firefly that landed on the windowsill and lit up right before him. When Joseph looked back up, she was gone.

Joseph had always wanted to believe in serendipity and that things happen for a reason. He wanted to believe in omens and signs. He wondered who this beautiful woman was and what she was trying to tell him. He pondered the dream she was in that revealed the insight to his sleep device, the dream that ultimately led him to this lab.

Joseph spent the next six months in his lab. He etched designs on his easel. He combined, mixed, and matched materials. He tested, experimented, and iterated. He breathed and dreamed.

PART II:

The Lab

After six months slaving in his lab, Joseph felt the only progress he'd made was burning a hole through his savings. The design was right, he knew it. The problem was the materials. Nothing seemed to work. The device was either too hard and metallic or too soft and unstable. He couldn't find the balance that he'd been searching for.

Joseph did a quick calculation in his head. Not a calculation for the device, but one to determine how much time he had left before he'd starve. He'd turned off the air conditioning already. He calculated that if he completely turned off the electricity, it would buy him one more month. He had no other option. He cut off the electricity. So much for having light.

With the electricity shut off, Joseph stopped working after sunset. He used to work through most nights. Now he spent that time staring out the one small window in his lab, watching his fireflies and trying to think through the solution to his material problem.

A week passed — still no closer to finding the right material.

He was low on money, low on food, and working in extreme heat. Nonetheless, over the last six months Joseph had more energy than he had ever had in his life. His head was clear. He had a freedom that he had not known before. He felt like he could do anything, that nothing could hold him back or weigh him down. However, his lack of income started to catch up. He had given himself six months of reserves to live on. Six months to create his sleep device. And six months were up. He cut every possible expense, rationed food, and saved every penny possible.

Joseph watched the fireflies at night. He wondered at their ability to carry their own source of light right inside their tiny bodies. He thought how useful it would be if he could provide his own internal source of light.

"What powers the fireflies' light?" Joseph pondered. If only he could tap into their source of light, he could keep working through the night and maybe prevent himself from starving. The bioluminescence of the firefly had stumped scientists for ages, though.

"I will come back to this thought." Joseph disciplined himself, trying not to be distracted from the task at hand — finding the material for his device.

Joseph drifted off to sleep, dreaming of the endless source of energy contained within the small bodies of his firefly friends.

‡

Per Joseph's calculation, he had two days left of food and no money. He also didn't have a solution to his materials problem.

Although he thought it was a long shot, Joseph saw no other option; he went to see his brother, Zachary, the banker.

"Hello, Joseph," Zachary said with a surprised look as he opened his door.

"Hi, Zach, how are you doing?" Joseph asked.

"I'm good. I wasn't expecting…"

"I know." Joseph cut him off. "I…"

"Come on in." Zach cut Joseph off this time. "Have a seat. What brings you?"

Zach led Joseph into his large living quarters. Gesturing for Joseph to take a seat on his fine leather couch, Zach perched back in his king-size recliner, arms propped up on his large stomach, fingers interlaced.

Joseph swallowed his pride getting straight to the point.

"Zach, I hate to ask this, but as you are a banker, I wanted to know if I could get a loan? Something just to get me by another month or two."

"Oh, Joseph, you aren't still working on that sleeping thing are you?" Zachary asked with a pleading shake of his head.

"I'm getting close. I can feel it. I know it." Joseph replied.

"Joseph, Joseph, Joseph. I'm sorry, but there is nothing I can do for you."

Joseph stared at his brother, waiting.

"You know you need collateral — something. I can't just give you money." Zach continued, "You need something to back it up."

Joseph slowly closed his eyes and continued to listen.

"You know, if you still had your practice or credibility as a doctor who could repay a debt, we could have a discussion. But you threw all that out on some whim, Joseph." Zach lectured as if he was a parent trying to give advice to a prodigal child.

"It was good to see you, Zach," Joseph said, as he stood up and walked to the door.

"You, too, Joseph. Take care of yourself. Forget this sleep thing. See if you can't get back on your feet as a doctor." Zach continued to lecture as Joseph shut the door behind him.

After being rejected by his brother and a long day in the heat inside, Joseph walked out to the small lake behind his lab. The sun was beginning to set, and he was going to have to stop working due to the darkness anyway.

Joseph sat on the edge, removed his shoes, and dropped his feet into the water. He lay back on the grass and watched the fireflies.

"Are you ok?"

A man popped up into Joseph's view, startling him. Joseph sat up and gathered himself. He was in no mood to lie to the stranger with fake optimism. At the same time, Joseph wasn't interested in conversation either.

"I'm ok for now," Joseph said.

The old man, sensing Joseph's reluctance for small talk, took a seat next to him. No words were spoken for some time. Joseph thought it was odd to be sitting with a stranger by a lake at sunset and not talking, but he didn't care much. He also thought it was strange that here he was, a doctor, with one day's worth of food left and no money.

"I've found that sometimes talking out loud helps clarify the talking on the inside." The old man finally broke the silence.

"I don't think relating my ills are going to help anything," Joseph replied.

"Try it."

Joseph relented and told the strange old man his story: He related how he had become a doctor and in his practice noticed the sleep problems of his patients. They were incessantly tired and depressed. He explained how he had stumbled upon a theory that it was due to their inability to dream, but his hypothesis was rejected by everyone — including his own brother. Regardless, he imagined this device that would enable people to dream again. He told the man how he had given up everything to create this device, but no material existed to get it to function. Now here he was with one day's food left, no money, no device, sitting by the lake with a strange old man.

The old man enjoyed Joseph's story.

"Do you mind if I see what you've done so far?" the old man asked.

"There's no use. I don't have any lights. I had to cut off the electricity. Plus, like I said, I only have one day's food left. I'm done."

And with these words, for the first time since leaving his practice and moving into his tiny apartment, Joseph's head pounded. The drumming was loud, fast, and relentless. He put his hands on the sides of his head and pressed on his temples.

No words were spoken for several minutes; or if the stranger had said something, Joseph couldn't hear it over the beating drum in his head.

"What could it hurt?" the old man persisted, "I have a flashlight. It's all we need."

"Fine." Joseph reluctantly agreed. "I need to go in and get something for this headache anyway."

Joseph led the old man to his apartment. It was a stifling 93 degrees in the stagnant lab, but the heat didn't seem to bother the old man. The drumming softened, but persisted in Joseph's head. He showed the old man the easel with his hundreds of sketches. He demonstrated his experimental trials with countless varieties of material combinations and design iterations. He pointed out on his massive periodic table how he chose element combinations and told of his struggle of not being able to uncover the right one. He told him how he thought something had to be missing. The old man just kept nodding, saying nothing.

"See? I'm at a dead end. Now if you don't mind, I'm not feeling great and would like to get some sleep," Joseph finished.

"Of course, I hope your head feels better in the morning." The stranger walked out the door into the dark of the night.

‡

The next morning, Joseph woke up to the drummer in his head. He had rationed his money and food over the last seven months, and he had arrived at the end. It was his last day of food. He decided he was going to sit and enjoy his last small food rationings and not think about the device. The thumping roared.

Joseph sat all day in his hot apartment wondering how he was going to survive. He could swallow his last bit of pride and beg for food and money from his parents. But he had become an embarrassment to them and thought he'd rather starve than face them as a beggar. He could try and get a job somewhere, but his skills were limited to treating patients. Reopening his practice was out of the question; he was seen as a charlatan who abandoned his patients on a cockamamie idea. The only thing he knew for sure was that he was through with his sleep device.

That night he finished his last meal and sat by his open window watching the fireflies as they lit up with their magical light.

As he began to drift off, Joseph heard a thump. At first he wasn't sure if it was his head or if someone was at the door.

"Hello?" Joseph said, half asleep.

"Hello, it's me, Abram, from last night. Do you have a minute?"

Abram? The strange old man? Joseph wondered as he staggered over to open the door.

"Sorry for coming by so late, but you were right; that was a tricky dilemma you were facing…it took me all day."

"What took you all day?" Joseph asked, puzzled.

"The material conundrum. But I think I got it!"

Joseph wondered if he was dreaming.

"Got it?"

"Yes. Come here. Let's take a look at your periodic table."

Abram pointed at the massive chart.

"You see silicone sitting here. You probably already know it's close to what you're looking for, but not exactly right. Aluminum and phosphorus sitting next to it are far too reactive — definitely not right. Germanium sitting below it is too hard. But then I looked more closely. It took me all day, but I was able to isolate silicone's children. Unfortunately, silicone's ten children aren't yet listed here on the periodic table. It made them a bit harder to find. But one of silicone's offspring I think will do the trick. It's a strong, resilient material, but it is also malleable and should be quite biocompatible."

"Wait. What? Am I dreaming?" Joseph now said aloud what he was thinking just a minute ago. "Silicone's children?"

"Of course you are; that is, if you're talking about a dream coming true! And yes, silicone has ten offspring, five males and five females, oppositely charged. Well, technically speaking, they are neon's children, the birthing element of the row, but they are split between silicone. Some scientists incorrectly refer to these as isotopes. The difficulty was these children hide under typical environmental conditions. That's what took me all day. I had to get the pressures just right in order to alter their dimensions to find them. A little game of hide and seek, if you will."

"But how…"

"You're familiar with the piano, right?" he asked rhetorically, to answer the question he assumed Joseph was going to ask.

"You see, the white keys on the piano are like the elements you see in that third row: sodium (Na), magnesium (Mg), aluminum (Al), silicone (Si), phosphorus (P), sulfur (S), chlorine (Cl), and argon (Ar). Now the white keys' tones are split by the black flat and sharp keys. I just found a way to find the sharps and flats that were hiding under silicone. And I think this new material is just what you're looking for!"

Abram showed Joseph how he could use the silicone he already had, alter its dimensions through changing potentials and pressures, and produce the sharps and flats of the third row of the periodic table.

For hours Joseph and the Abram molded this new "element" into the designs that were created in Joseph's imagination over a year ago. It was just as Abram predicted. This new material was strong, yet soft and functional, and appeared to be perfectly biocompatible.

They worked all night together. After they had created twelve devices, Abram departed.

‡

Joseph's calculations were correct. He was out of food and out of money. But his energy was back. The drumming in his head was gone. He was ready to give his gift to the world. He thought of his patient Tom and smiled with a thankful nod as if Tom was there watching in approval.

In a couple boxes stored away in the corner of the lab, Joseph had some of his old patient records with names and addresses. He flipped through them and found twelve patients who had suffered from fatigue and depression.

With their addresses in hand and zero hours of sleep, Joseph headed out.

He arrived at his first address. Joseph knocked. His former patient slowly dragged himself to the door, looked through the peephole, and opened the door with a bewildered look on his face.

"Dr. Joseph?" he asked as if it took all the energy he could muster. "What are you doing here?"

"I have something for you," Joseph said. "Are you still suffering from fatigue and depression?"

"What does it look like?" the man sarcastically replied.

"It looks like I may have your answer," Joseph said. "Wear this tonight."

"What is it?" the man asked, looking at the device suspiciously.

"It's a device designed to help you start dreaming again," Joseph explained.

The lethargic man took the device, gave Joseph a non-confirming nod, and shut the door. It wasn't the warmest welcome. Perhaps it was because Joseph had shut down his practice rather abruptly. Nonetheless, Joseph was thrilled to get his device into the hands of his first patient.

Joseph continued on to the next address and then the next one after that.

After countless miles of traveling, Joseph arrived at the twelfth and final address. He had one last device to give.

He knocked. From behind the opening door, the eyes that had captured his months ago were peering at him. It was the woman by the lake, the woman from his dream.

"Hello." Her eyes smiled. Joseph lost his breathe, and his train of thought went with it.

"Hi…"

Silence.

"Can I help you?" she asked.

"Hi. Yes. Sorry. I'm Joseph. I'm here to give something to Ethan."

"That's my father. I'll tell him you're here. May I ask what brings you?"

"Yes, I have something to give him that I believe will help his sleep."

She smiled knowingly and disappeared into the house. As she turned to get her father, the flow of her hair was unmistakable; it was the girl he couldn't catch in his dream, the same girl out by the lake behind his lab.

"Hey, Dr. Joseph, how have you been?" a large man groaned as he approached the door.

"Hi, Ethan, I have something for you." Joseph got straight to the point, handing Ethan the device that had nearly brought him to starvation.

Ethan inspected the device suspiciously.

"So this is supposed to help me sleep?"

"Yes, it should allow you to dream again," Joseph explained.

Ethan nodded and thanked Joseph with an insincere hand-shake. He shut the door, inspected the strange device in his hand, and tossed it into the waste basket.

"Dream? What a joke."

Joseph made his way back to his apartment, oblivious to his thirst and hunger. He sat up all night, looking out his window. He watched the fireflies put on their nightly fire-works display.

Just as the sun started to peek over the horizon, Joseph was finally able to shut his eyes and fall asleep. Over the last two days he had no sleep and hardly any food or wa-ter, but was powered from an infinite energy within.

He had done it.

He created a device that the world had never known; he reveled in bringing his inspiration and imagination to life.

Joseph slept for the next three days.

‡

When Joseph finally awoke, the world felt different. He felt like he'd stepped out of one life into a completely new world — one filled with limitless possibilities. The world was brighter; it felt lighter; it felt free.

Joseph opened his front door to go in search of some much-needed food. As he took a step out the door, he kicked a pile of envelopes that covered his doormat.

He picked them up and brought them to his workbench. He opened the first one which was dated three days ago:

Dr. Joseph,

Yesterday, I have to admit, it was quite strange to see you. After abruptly closing the doors to your practice and with the talk around the town, I didn't think I'd see you again. Forgive me for my impertinence when you handed me some device that I had never seen before. But as you know, I have suffered for years from crippling fatigue and depression. So even though I was skeptical, I was quite willing to try anything. Last night I slept with the device and had dreams like I couldn't even begin to explain! They were vivid, exciting, and lively! I woke up feeling rejuvenated, feeling like a new man! I've had so much energy today that I literally ran here to thank you, to hug you, to kiss

you if you'd let me! I banged on your door for
nearly twenty minutes but figured you weren't
home. So I wrote you this letter to say THANK
YOU. I wanted to leave you a little something as
well to try and express my gratitude.

Thank you Dr. Joseph!

-Your forever indebted, energetic patient

Joseph looked into the envelope. He could hardly believe it. It contained more money than he used to make in a month at his practice. He opened the next letter also dated three days ago. It was another note of gratitude. More money poured out. The next envelope held the same message and more money. There were a total of eleven envelopes, all praising Joseph for his genius. The envelopes contained money totaling more than he had made in all his days in his practice combined. One of the envelopes had an invitation for dinner, which sounded mighty good to Joseph right about this time.

Joseph was ecstatic, yet at the same time wondered about the twelfth patient, Ethan.

"Did it not work?"

Joseph had delivered twelve devices and received eleven letters, so he easily deduced that it was Ethan who had not responded. Although he had not expected any responses, the fact that he heard from eleven of the twelve made him worry about Ethan. He would inquire of him later. But first he needed to get some food. It had been ages since he last ate a good meal. His pants were getting loose, and his shirt baggy.

Joseph walked down the street into the city with his destination already decided. Since moving to the outskirts of the city, there was a place that he had always wanted to eat, but couldn't justify spending the money. That was no longer an issue.

As Joseph arrived at the diner, a hand gently grabbed his wrist from behind him. The fingers brushed against his palm and sent an electric current through his body. Goosebumps sprung up, and the hair on his arms and the back of his neck rose.

"Joseph." The sweet sound of her voice was as if spoken by an angel.

Joseph turned to be enraptured by the eyes that had drawn him in twice before.

"I'm sorry. I didn't mean to startle you," the woman apologized, mistakenly thinking that Joseph's breath being taken away was from scaring him. "I have been trying to find you. I've stopped at your address the last three days, but no one has answered."

Joseph just smiled. No words came to him. His three-day coma would be hard to explain anyway.

"I've been trying to give you this." She handed Joseph a small, nicely wrapped box.

"Thank you," Joseph said, finally able to speak. "Would you like to have breakfast with me?"

The woman smiled.

They sat down for breakfast. Even though Joseph's appetite had been stolen by the angel sitting in front of him, he knew his body was in much need of nutrition.

"What's in the box?" Joseph asked.

"Open it and see."

Joseph smiled, happy to comply.

As he tore the paper wrapping back, he wondered what could possibly be inside. As he lifted the lid off the box, Joseph was struck by a golden light.

Inside the box was a necklace with a small, golden drum dangling from the end. Joseph couldn't tell if it was reflecting light or radiating it. It was beautiful.

"My father, Ethan, use to be a great drummer." She began to explain. "When he was younger, he was known throughout much of the world for his musical abilities. Great crowds would come to hear him play. He drummed like no one else before him.

"At first his style was ridiculed by the older musicians. Many thought he must be deaf to beat on the drums the way he did. But my father heard the drum not with his outer eardrum, but with his inner ear. When I was little, he always told me to 'march to the beat of your drum.' He even nicknamed me Yourdrum and gave me this necklace as a constant reminder. We want to give to you."

Joseph didn't know what to say, "I can't possibly accept..."

She took the necklace and put it around his neck.

"Several years ago, my father was in an accident where he was badly injured. His right hand was crushed," she continued, as she secured the necklace around Joseph. "His heart crushed with it. He stopped playing the drums. He started getting tired and depressed.

"Before the accident, he told me he wanted to teach others to drum the way he knew to drum; to hear the way he could hear. Following his accident, I tried to tell him to continue his dream of teaching others his talents. Initially, he told me he would when he felt ready. Time passed, and he did nothing. When I would question him, he would get angry. One day, he scolded me severely. He grabbed me and shouted that I was to never bring up the idea again. I have obeyed his wishes and watched his life deteriorate into a lifeless existence. Until a couple days ago, I had given up hope for him. After you delivered the device, he threw it into the wastebasket. But something told me that this was his answer. When my father went to sleep that night, I pulled it out of the trash and put it on him. The next morning, the man who awoke was the father I knew many years ago. There was a light in his eyes, a bounce in his step, and an energy that pulsed from him. I confessed what I did, and he broke down crying, thanking me for my help. I am here now to thank you for your help."

Joseph's eyes welled and his throat swelled. He cleared his throat searching for words.

"Your father hadn't dreamed for a long time; it's understandable that he was tired and depressed. I'm very happy the device worked for him. But still I can't possibly…" Joseph responded holding the golden drum in his fingers.

She cut him off, continuing, "Yesterday, he pulled out his old drums that had been collecting dust in the closet for years. Watching him drum to his beat was a heavenly sight and sound."

At that, the girl smiled, stood up, and started walking toward the door.

"Wait, I didn't get your name…" Joseph said, wanting to keep her from leaving.

She looked back with a grin, "Yourdrum."

‡

Joseph spent the rest of the day returning to his patients' houses where he made the deliveries just three days before to thank them for their letters and money.

House after house, the patients swung their doors open, embraced the young doctor, and cried tears of joy — tears of life.

Joseph's last stop was at Mr. Henry's house, which was the patient who offered a dinner invitation. After months of rationing food, he was ready for his second good meal of the day.

Sitting on seven acres, Mr. Henry's house was the largest in town, truly one of a kind. As Joseph strode up the long walkway to the front of the house, Mr. Henry opened the door, shouting for Joseph to come in.

Mr. Henry embraced Joseph exclaiming, "Doctor, you are my savior!"

While still in an embrace, Mr. Henry ordered, "Come. Let's celebrate with a feast!"

And a feast it was. With innumerable entrees, Joseph didn't know where to start. He piled his plate high. Over dinner Mr. Henry couldn't stop raving about the device; how wonderful his sleep had been the last three nights and how he felt like a new man. Mrs. Henry commented on his renewed energy, vitality, and drive. It was like he was 20-years-old again. He was even wearing her out. Joseph blushed.

Joseph ate more in this meal than he had in the last six months combined. And that was before they brought the pie out.

Over dessert, Mr. Henry got down to business.

"Doctor, do you know what I do?"

Joseph shook his head as he swallowed a large piece of pie.

"I am what people call a *merger*," he explained. "My job is to aid businesses in finding partners to help them both grow. I merge businesses together. It's a business strategy based on synergy. Do you know what synergy is?"

"Yes," Joseph said. "That's when a total is greater than the sum of its parts."

"Absolutely right. I find businesses that, when brought together, are stronger as one than either is alone."

"That must be a very rewarding job," Joseph said, smiling.

"Well, it was early in my career. I learned a lot and made a lot of money. But it has been a drag the last several years. For quite some time, I considered quitting the job to start my own business; but the money was too good to leave, so I stayed. That was until three days ago when you gave me your device. My life has changed. My energy, drive, and ambition to create returned!"

"That is wonderful!" Joseph happily remarked. "What kind of business are you going to start?"

"A business that enables a man to dream again! I want to buy your invention from you and start a business that can distribute this miracle device to the world. I want people to wake up and feel like I did this morning! Of course, that's only if you want to sell it."

A thrill pierced through Joseph. He smiled, thinking of Tom.

"That's the reason I made it — to give it to the world," Joseph explained, remembering what his fancy-dressing patient had told him seemingly ages ago.

Mr. Henry nodded approvingly, "Then let's look at some numbers, shall we?"

Joseph and Mr. Henry negotiated a deal that made Joseph a very wealthy man. He had the money to do whatever he wanted for the rest of his life.

Mr. Henry went about getting Joseph's sleep device into the hands of every tired, depressed, non-dreaming person in the land. He unleashed his drive to create, which he had long buried away. With his new found vitality, combined with his business expertise, he wheeled and dealed. Before long, every hospital, clinic, and doctor was prescribing Joseph's sleep device.

The results proved to be extraordinary.

Life expectancy increased, disease and illness plummeted, and the world's economy was stimulated into unprecedented growth with the mass adoption of Joseph's invention. People were dreaming.

‡

As Mr. Henry expanded the business, Joseph's fame increased. Doctors sought his advice, his presence was requested throughout the land, and people everywhere praised his genius.

The friends and colleagues who had turned their backs on Joseph and his naïve idea and cockamamie theory now requested his presence at dinners, on trips and vacations, and in their social circles.

Joseph's family was proud to be seen with him in public again. His parents gloated over their son's audacity and brilliance. His older brother, the renowned surgeon, boasted of his family's medical prowess. His two younger brothers, the lawyer and banker, applauded how wise he was and admired his mountain of wealth. Zachary, ironically, was happy to loan him money whenever he needed it.

Joseph loved feeling wanted again. He loved feeling important. He loved his mountain of money. He loved having the admiration and respect of the world.

Over the coming months, Joseph built a house — known as the castle — that made Mr. Henry's look like a doll house. Joseph hired an army of caretakers to look after the house, prepare feasts, entertain guests, and pamper him day and night.

Shortly after the construction of his castle, Joseph sought the assistance of his staff to find his "dream girl," the woman from the diner who gifted him his brilliant, gold necklace.

She was nowhere to be found.

‡

Joseph enjoyed living big.

His castle, lavish parties, and worry-free life were wonderful. Yet, secretly, Joseph fought a restless undercurrent, a drumming that beat on his heartstrings.

When Joseph tired of spending time in his castle, he had a pool built the size of a lake. He lounged out by the pool daily, soaking in the sun. Not long after, becoming restless from endless hours lounging poolside, Joseph decided to travel the world collecting rare rubies and jewels to put on display in his castle. Country after country, continent after continent, Joseph sought the rarest of metals, coins, jewels, and rubies. He purchased these with reckless abandon. He showcased them throughout the castle. The scintillating décor of his castle was magnificent. Yet, in time, even the chase of jewels lost its allure.

Joseph could feel a hole that clamored to be filled. He turned to food to appease the disquiet, to fill the emptiness. The most exquisite dishes from around the world were delivered to his master table in his grand dining hall. Feasts ensued nightly.

When the distraction of food stopped appeasing his restless heart, Joseph became a wine connoisseur. Bottles aged for hundreds of years were gulped down in minutes. His blood swam with equal mixtures of alcohol and water throughout most days.

He started to get headaches in the morning, thumping inside his skull. He drank more wine to quiet the drumming.

Joseph began to feel tired.

"Lots of wine and food make a man tired. It's normal, and I've earned it," Joseph justified to himself.

The drumming headaches and fatigue worsened. Joseph turned to women to revitalize him. Night after night new women entered his master bedroom. Blonde, brunette, tall, short, dark skinned and light skinned. But in time, even the women lost their appeal. The more Joseph sought to fill the hole within, the larger it grew.

"Something is missing here."

The thought that struck Joseph ages ago had been haunting him in between wine binges and female entertainment. He tried to ignore it.

"What could be missing? I have everything a man could ever want." Joseph thought. *"I have wealth, fame, women, and butlers to care for me; nothing is missing."*

With that thought, the drumming in his head picked up. Joseph reached for another bottle of wine.

‡

One morning, a butler brought in a package addressed to Joseph. In it was a note from Mr. Henry.

> *Joseph, I hope you are doing well! I'm sending you this letter for two reasons.*
>
> *First, I owe you another thank you — now and forever. You have changed my life and enabled me to create a business that has changed the lives of countless people! Thank you!*
>
> *The creation which you brought forth from your lab is a true testament to the power one man can use to change the world.*
>
> *Secondly, I received word from a mutual friend of ours. He's a strange old man, but he said you may need your own genius. He also said he would love to see you in your lab again.*
>
> *Much love,*
>
> *Mr. Henry*

He turned the envelope over and a sleep device fell into Joseph's hand. As he looked at his creation, Joseph realized he hadn't dreamed in months.

That night Joseph put aside his pride and tried out his device for the first time.

‡

The next morning, Joseph jumped out of bed. He was still a young man, but for the first time in a long time, actually felt it. No drumming. No fogginess. His mind was clear, open, like it was transparent to the world. Energy pulsed through his veins; drive seeped from his pores.

"This device really is amazing." Joseph patted himself on the back.

Joseph dressed and made his own breakfast. The cook wondered what was wrong and feared losing her job.

"Sir, is everything ok?" she timidly asked.

"Of course, take the morning off," Joseph replied with a smile. It was the first time she had ever seen Joseph's real smile.

After breakfast, Joseph went out back and instead of lounging by the pool, swam in it for the first time. As he exercised, he thought back to Mr. Henry's letter.

> *"The creation which you brought forth from your lab is a true testament to the power one man can use to change the world…"*

"And, who is this mutual friend, this strange old man?" Joseph wondered. *"Surely not THE strange old man, Abram…"*

"What did he mean? What was he trying to say? Why would I go back to that old lab?" Joseph didn't understand. The lab was pure hell. It was an unrelenting furnace. It was solitude. It was struggle.

Yet, in the lab Joseph had never been more free or alive in his life.

"Maybe I should get back in the lab…but why?" He wasn't sure.

The device rejuvenated him for the day.

That night, sitting on his king-size bed in deep thought, one of his favorite women knocked and peeked in. The olive-skinned beauty held a bottle of Joseph's favorite wine. Joseph looked at the woman and then glanced over to his sleep device. With a wave of his hand, he signaled the woman to enter; and he tucked his sleep device away into the drawer of the nightstand.

Several weeks passed. His sleep device remained hidden in his nightstand's drawer. The hole within grew deeper. He continued trying to fill it by drowning it with excess. He wanted more. He wanted *gold*.

‡

Adjacent to Joseph's castle was a large plot of land. He decided it was the perfect spot. He wasn't sure who owned it, so the next morning Joseph set out to meet his neighbor. The land owner was a rugged, strong-looking man who wore a long beard. He was tilling his land when Joseph approached.

"Hi there, my name is Joseph. I live next door and couldn't help but admire the great piece of land you have here."

"Thank you," the rugged man replied, glancing up from his work. Joseph's golden necklace caught his eye. "So, how can I help you?" he asked as he went back to his work.

"I was wondering if you'd be willing to sell this property?" Joseph asked, foregoing small talk.

The bearded land owner thought it over for less than a minute.

"Ok." The rugged man replied without looking up.

The land wasn't cheap, but Joseph didn't care. He bought it that day, because it was the perfect spot for his new lab. The deal agreed upon called for Joseph to make monthly payments until the entire property was paid for. If for any reason payment was delinquent, the rugged man would retain the property.

With the property secured, Joseph sought out the best architects in the world who designed a science lab fit for a king. The drawings detailed a building unlike any before. With the blueprints in hand, Joseph hired builders to construct his new lab — the Science Center Institute (SCI).

It was magnificent. It had no equal. Joseph furnished the lab with state-of-the-art instruments, technology, and equipment. Joseph ordered the best materials from around the world. He gathered the elements from the periodic table in their purest forms. After spending much of his fortune, the Science Center Institute was set.

His plan was almost ready. All he needed now were the scientists to execute his idea.

Joseph gathered the most renowned scientists in the world and brought them to the SCI.

After days of deliberation with the brightest scientific minds in the world in the most magnificent lab the world had known, a team was formed that agreed to obey Joseph's commands — attempt to master the age old art of alchemy, transmuting base metals into gold.

Those who deemed it impossible, Joseph ordered to leave. Those who silenced their doubts, Joseph hired.

"With these brilliant, scientific minds and the magnificent SCI, surely we can uncover the secret of transforming base metals into gold," Joseph assured himself, justifying his spending of the majority of his remaining wealth. *"Then I will truly have it all with limitless gold."*

The scientists went to work. They labored for weeks.

The famous Russian chemist struggled day and night trying to remove an electron from mercury. But no matter what method he employed, he wasn't able to pluck an electron out, not even from the largest orbitals that loosely held onto their electrons.

Weeks turned into months. Still no luck.

Not one metal was even remotely transmuted into another. Joseph's mountain of wealth had whittled down to a small mound. He cursed the scientists for their stupidity and lack of results. Joseph thought back to Abram who was able to uncover a new material element in one day. Joseph wondered how he could find him.

"Surely," Joseph thought, *"the old man could produce gold in no time."*

As the days continued to pass, the money continued to diminish. Joseph spent less and less time in the SCI and more time with his wine and women.

‡

After spending the morning poolside with a bottle of wine, Joseph made his way to the SCI to check on the scientists. He was shocked to see no one there. Joseph turned red with rage.

"Where is everyone?" Joseph shouted. "I pay these scientists a fortune!" he roared.

The chief caretaker of the SCI explained to Joseph that the scientists had left.

"Why did they leave?" Joseph asked in a low, slow voice, trying to contain his anger.

"Sir, there is no more money to pay them. So they left."

"No more money? How is that possible?"

Joseph stormed out in a fit.

Not long after the scientists departed, payments could no longer be made to maintain the SCI. Joseph had spent his fortune building the palace and wasn't about to let it go.

"I have rubies and jewels to make this month's payment," Joseph bargained. The rugged man was reluctant. According to their deal, he would reclaim ownership if Joseph failed to uphold their agreed upon monthly price.

"Joseph, why don't you let me buy the land back from you, and you go back to your home?" the rugged man suggested.

Joseph insisted. The rugged man relented and accepted his jewels. Joseph had bought himself more time.

Alone in his magnificent lab, Joseph didn't know where to start. He wished he had spent more time in the SCI when the scientists were there experimenting. At least then he would know what not to do.

Time passed without any progress. The ancient secrets of alchemy remained.

Not long after his prior visit, the rugged man returned to reclaim his land and the SCI with it. He found Joseph sprawled on the floor with an empty wine bottle under his arm, propping up his head like a pillow.

"Working hard I see," the rugged man said as he bent down and shook Joseph's shoulder. Joseph awoke with a loud gasp. Rubbing his eyes, Joseph recognized the rugged man standing over him. The monthly payment was due, and Joseph had no means to pay it.

Joseph begged the man, offering him wine and women, but he had no interest in his wine or women. Joseph was desperate. He anguished at the thought of losing his SCI. He looked around the lab for something — anything — to offer the man.

A glitter of gold caught his eye — the golden drum that hung from his neck. Hastily unhooking it, Joseph held it out to the man.

The rugged man looked at the necklace with a sense of familiarity. He held the drum between his fingers, studying it as if trying to recall a memory. With a nod, he reluctantly accepted.

"You have bought yourself one more month. If you are unable to continue payment at that time, this land and your Science Center Institute are mine."

Joseph agreed.

Joseph, with no faith in himself, believed he needed someone else's help in order to uncover the secrets of alchemy. He went searching for the strange old man, Abram.

‡

Joseph spent his last month continuing his search outside himself. He feared looking within to the one person who could save him. He had a complete lack of belief in himself. He had hoped someone would come to the rescue and save his SCI...save him. But no one came.

One month passed. No Abram. No gold. No money.

Joseph lost his land and the SCI with it.

In despair Joseph retreated to his castle. But without money to pay his caretakers, they, too, left. The women stopped coming. The wine cellar dried out.

Even his castle was taken from him as he could no longer afford the taxes.

Joseph had no money, no food, no place to live. The friends and family that enjoyed his riches were nowhere to be found.

Joseph sat on the street curb outside his castle and wept.

‡

"It's kind of late to be out sitting on the street, isn't it?" a familiar voice in the dark asked.

Joseph looked up and recognized the rugged man.

"I guess this is rock bottom," Joseph replied, putting his head back into his hands.

The man smiled knowingly.

"Rock bottom can be a powerful place if you let it. Most people never have the luxury of experiencing rock bottom."

"The luxury?" Joseph shot him a dubious look. "How do you mean?"

The rugged man took a seat next to Joseph.

"At rock bottom, fear can no longer control your life. You have nothing to lose. When you hit rock bottom, it's an opportunity to retake the reins of your life. Instead of letting fear control it, you dictate your life. Because you have only two options," the rugged man said, holding two fingers out. "You can stay there or you can climb up; and as long as you choose not to stay there, then you can only go up."

"Interesting point of view," Joseph said, not feeling any better from the philosophy lesson.

The rugged man continued to relate his esoteric philosophy on life.

"The real interesting point of view is when you realize no matter what you have, you don't have anything to lose."

Sensing that Joseph needed further explanation, the rugged man pressed on.

"Do you have time for a story?" he asked Joseph, who had buried his face in his hands again.

"Time?" Joseph replied as he looked up. "That is the *only* thing I have."

Joseph welcomed a distraction from his misery.

"Great." The rugged man said as he launched into the story.

"Once there was this young boy. He grew up in a privileged household, a well-respected family in the community. The young boy grew up with what any child could hope for — loving parents, the best education, friends, and a bright future by anyone's account. When the boy turned of age, his father expected to pass down the family business to him, grow the family legacy, and ensure a safe and secure future for his young son. But there was a problem."

"I don't see any problem." Joseph interrupted.

The rugged man smiled.

"The young boy was curious. He was restless. He had a nagging desire for adventure. He wanted to travel the world. He wanted to see where other people lived, what they did, immerse in other cultures and languages, and explore lands, seas, and mountains. His parents didn't understand. His father tried explaining that people travel from long distances to live where they live, to have the luxuries they have, and to enjoy the highest quality and standard of living that they enjoy. His mother pleaded that there was no better place on earth to find a wife, raise children, and live prosperously.

"They didn't understand. Neither wealth nor comfort could satisfy the boy's heart. Without his parents blessing, he took off with nothing but a small backpack with water and a little food.

"The boy travelled for several weeks with his limited resources. Finding food and water for survival was a daily endeavor. As his supplies ran out, he found himself in a strange town. He wasn't sure where he was or even what direction he had headed. In this town, the young boy came upon some men building a house. He asked if he could help in exchange for food and water. The boy knew nothing of building houses, but he was young and strong. The head-man leading the construction accepted his offer.

"The boy learned how to erect walls, lay floors, and construct roofs. He awoke before dawn and worked until sunset. It was hot, the sun blazed in the afternoons; but the boy powered on. Night after night the boy slept out in the open air with his backpack as a pillow. The head-man admired the young boy's work ethic and began paying him. The money allowed the young boy to rent a small room. Sleeping on a normal bed with a regular pillow, the young boy was able to work even harder and quickly rose to be one of the favorites of the head-man. He was awarded a large raise and was allowed to take one day off every week.

"On his day off and in the evenings, the young boy wandered through the town. He became friends with the locals; he learned their customs and past times. He frequently joined in the music festivities and wine tasting. He was well liked by all. The town and his work had become comfortable.

"About this time, the boy began to feel it again. It was the same feeling he had back in his hometown. It was a drumming feeling in his heart and in his head. The boy knew it was time to move on. The head-man urged him to stay, to keep building. He offered the boy another raise in pay, another day off. When the boy declined, the head-man offered him a partnership in the business to stay. He offered him his own home. When the head-man realized nothing he could offer could get the boy to stay, he relented and told him that if he ever wandered back to this town, his door was always open. The boy thanked him, said his goodbyes, and headed off. Watching the boy leave town, the head-man felt like he was losing a son.

"The boy had savings that enabled him to travel further. He sailed to Greece. He walked the sands of the Greek islands and soaked up the salt of the sea. He proceeded to Italy. It was there that his savings began to run dry. To others, it would appear he was at rock bottom again — no home, no family, no possessions."

"I can relate to that," Joseph interjected.

"But the boy didn't see it that way," the rugged man continued. "Exploring Italy, the boy noticed beautiful, un-inhabited parcels of land. He thought how wonderful it would be for people to live in these beautiful hills of Italy. He counted his money. He had just enough to buy the necessary supplies. He began building. He completed his first house all by himself, from the floors to the walls to the roof. In need of money, he sold it to a family of four.

"The family was so impressed with the house that their oldest son joined the boy in building more homes. The boy taught the son how to build a house properly. As they built, more people joined the boy's growing business. The boy built himself a beautiful house in the hills of Italy. By now, he had become wealthy and known as the finest builder in Italy. He loved Italy. He enjoyed the wines, pas-tas, and walks in the towns. He loved his home in the hills and the beautiful women that seemed to populate the area. He was friends with the locals, as well as the tourists and fellow travelers whom he frequently entertained in his home. The boy was comfortable. And he began to hear it again. Thump, thump, thump. It was the drum, the beat of desire to continue on, to explore.

"A newly-married couple admired and much desired the boy's house in the hills of Italy; however, they couldn't afford to buy a house of such grandeur in the beautiful hills, which had become the area's most desired location. The boy and the couple came to an agreement. If and when he ever returned to Italy, there would always be a room for him. The whole of Italy all but begged him to stay. But the boy set out.

"His drum brought him to the mountains next. He relished the beauty of the snow-capped giants. Again, the boy employed his survival skills. While in the mountains, he struck up a friendship with an older man who shared his adventurous, risk-taking spirit. The older man was vacationing in the mountains for some peace and rejuvenation, as well as adventure and excitement. The older man was enthralled by the boy's stories and his travels and impressed with his boldness and self-reliance. Before departing back to his home, the older man tried to recruit the boy to come work with him in his business. He offered the boy an unfathomable salary. But he wasn't ready yet. His drum told him to keep going.

"The boy went to Africa, India, China, France, Spain. He explored the Americas. He went around the equator and to the arctic poles. Everywhere he went, he learned, grew, gave, and then continued."

"I'm not sure I'm getting the point." Joseph interrupted the story.

"The boy traveled the world," the rugged man continued, ignoring Joseph's interruption. "One day, many years later, he returned home. His parents barely recognized him. He had grown into a man. He spoke fourteen languages. He was a master builder, farmer, fisherman, and hunter. He was learned in every culture imaginable. His parents looked at him and scolded their son.

"'Look, we warned you,' they said. 'You are now a grown man with no money and no home and no family.'

"The son smiled. He had riches throughout the world, a home in every land, and family in every walk of life. He was free. He was welcome anywhere in the world. He had mastered every craft of survival, growth, and utility. But most of all, his heart was satisfied; his drummer was singing."

"So what happened to the boy?" Joseph asked.

"His drum brought him back home where he bought land and continued the trades he learned throughout the world. He found peace in farming, hunting, fishing, and building. He found the love of his life. They started a family. He enjoyed a full life toiling his land, teaching his children, and loving his wife."

"And let me guess; he lived happily ever after…" Joseph quipped.

"Well, that's still to be determined."

"What do you mean?" Joseph curiously asked. "So this is a true story?"

"Sure is," the rugged man replied. "Today this man also works as the chief advisor to a very large business. This business provides electricity to the majority of the world. The inventor and owner of this business found a way to conduct electricity with half the waste of prior methods. The inventor is considered a genius, as well as the wealthiest man alive. Rumor has it that he is also a good man. After his discovery of low waste, low-cost electricity, he offered his solution to his competitors through a licensing agreement. He knew it would be impossible for them to compete with this new technology. Instead of putting them all out of business, he wanted to offer a solution to keep all the businesses operating and people employed by structuring collaborative relationships with his would-be competitors. It was a more-than-fair deal. People inside his company thought he was crazy. But the competitors resisted. They feared collaboration and opted for competition. Well, they couldn't compete. The inventor's business wiped out nearly every competitor. The only survivors were those wise enough to finally join forces before being forced out.

"How could a traveling boy get such a job?" Joseph asked incredulously.

"Remember the older man he met in the mountains, the one who shared a common fearless spirit?"

"The one who was vacationing…" Joseph connected the dots.

"When the boy returned from his travels, he had the job waiting for him. The older man's company needed someone who understood different cultures and needs. The boy's yearly salary to advise the inventor was more than most make in a lifetime."

"Perhaps I should go vacationing in the mountains," Joseph joked, lightening up for the first time in a long time. "Where is this traveler now?"

"Well, one day, a desperate sounding man needed some of his land, one of his favorite plots. The traveling boy, who was now a man with a family, didn't want to sell his prized lot, but the drummer inside mysteriously told him to. He had learned to listen to the drum. So he sold it.

"However, through some unfortunate circumstances, the buyer could no longer make payments on the land. The traveler had to reclaim his plot that now boasted a large building right in the middle of his hunting ground."

Joseph paused and looked at the rugged man.

"The boy…the traveler is…" Joseph started.

With that, the rugged traveler patted Joseph on his knee, stood up, and walked off into the dark.

Lying back in the grass, Joseph looked up at the stars and thought of the rugged man's travels, his boldness, his fearlessness to live *his* life. Joseph started to draw the parallels from the rugged man's story and his own life. As a boy, the rugged man left behind a secure future in his family's business against the discretion of all those around him. Similarly, Joseph had left behind his safe future as a doctor to create his sleep device. Both had the courage to listen to their hearts, to follow their dreams. However, there was a noted difference. The rugged man kept going, kept growing, kept giving.

As Joseph began to understand the rugged man's message, he saw fireflies.

He hadn't seen them in ages. They calmed him. He watched. He listened.

Watching the golden glow pour out of the fireflies, Joseph wondered what his drum would tell him now. And no sooner did he ask, did the answer arrive.

"Go to *your* lab."

The thought reverberated in his head. It was as if someone put the thought in there and wouldn't let it escape. Or, maybe the fireflies learned to communicate. Or, perhaps, he learned to understand them.

Joseph headed back to his lab.

‡

Walking down the dark street, Joseph wasn't angry or sad anymore. The loss of his riches, his castle, his SCI, his butlers, food, wine, and women felt like a heavy weight had been lifted from his shoulders. He felt light.

The hole that he struggled so mightily to fill closed up.

He had crossed the threshold from fear to freedom.

Joseph thought back to the last time he crossed this chasm. He had given up his practice, his safe and secure income, his "Dr.," his respect among friends, family, and colleagues. In letting it all go, he had gained infinitely more. He gained freedom.

On his walk back to his lab, he remembered his first time finding this freedom. It took courage, strength, and conviction. This time, it seemed the world had forced his hand. Perhaps that was the world's reward for taking the first leap on his own; it made the next one easier or down right forced it upon him.

PART III:

Fireflies

When Joseph arrived at his long lost lab, he knocked, wondering what lucky fool was living there now.

No answer.

Joseph knocked again.

Nothing.

Joseph turned the knob of the door and was surprised to find it unlocked.

"Hello?"

Silence.

Joseph walked in. His lab remained just as he had left it. He felt a strange sensation of being at home. He had never had that feeling at the castle or the Science Center Institute. Joseph figured that no one could ever take your true home from you. He delighted in the heat.

Faint beams from the rising sun shone through the lone, small window. His periodic table still hung covering the wall above his workbench. His easel stood in the corner with hundreds of design renditions of the device that had made him fortunes. Home again at last.

Light filled the lab.

That day Joseph went straight to work. He cleaned up the easel, putting up fresh white pages ready to be imagined on. He sat studying his periodic table, relearning atomic masses, the rotations and revolution patterns, the gravitation and radiation forces of the elements of the world. Joseph recalled studying all this ages ago in school. At that time, he had tried to soak all this information in. Now, Joseph felt that he was releasing that which was already inside, that which he had buried and sealed. He pried the lid open. Knowledge that was long trapped seeped into his open mind.

Joseph mapped out the elements on the fresh paper on his easel. Just as Abram had taught him that talking aloud could help clarify a thought, Joseph believed so could writing it out. It was like casting a fishing hook into the deep waters and catching the idea, bringing it to the surface with clarity of form.

Time passed in the lab without notice.

Sitting against the wall, arms crossed around his knees, Joseph was half staring at his periodic table, half searching the inner depths of his mind. The same feeling came to him that struck him ages ago in his lab.

"Something is missing here."

As the sun set, he stared out the open window, admiring his tiny, flying friends that were putting on their beautiful light display. When in his lab, the fireflies always came to light up his night. As he sat watching, a firefly descended like a dove into his palm. As it touched his hand, its body lit up. A thought Joseph had ages ago popped into his head.

"What powers the firefly's light?"

Joseph felt a drumming in his heart, an urge to explore this unsolved mystery. He looked at his periodic table on the wall. It hit him in a flash — yes, something *was* missing — the light of the firefly.

He jumped from his seat on the windowsill and went for his flashlight. Focusing its beam on the periodic table, Joseph studied the chart of elements, asking it where it was incomplete.

He decided the best place to start was from what he knew. He grabbed his easel and put it closer to the chart.

From his early chemistry study, Joseph knew the basic ingredients of bioluminescence. It was like a recipe of oxygen, hydrogen, nitrogen, and other elements mixed in with luciferin, a substrate that converts to oxyluciferin via a special enzyme called luciferase. Also added to the recipe was some energy in the form of ATP to make all the ingredients come together in the right way.

The problem was this reaction shouldn't work.

Chemically speaking, the recipe ingredients shouldn't mix.

"So how is this reaction happening?" Joseph wondered, deep in thought.

Joseph grabbed a pencil.

He wrote out the chemical reaction as taught in school. He mapped out the luciferin and its bond with oxygen catalyzed by luciferase and ATP. He diagramed the products of oxyluciferin and emitted photons of light. He drew arrows showing how electrons would have to be combined, shared, and released.

He had a moment of gratitude for his wonderful, organic chemistry teacher, Dr. Moodie.

Joseph took a seat on his workbench, propped his head up with his hand, and shook his head. It just couldn't work.

"There has to be something missing. A missing step. A missing element…"

For this reaction to work, the oxygen would have to behave against the principles of nature. The oxygen would have to carry an extra electron. This was unlikely. Even if it did somehow carry this extra electron, it would be super reactive — like dropping pure sodium into water. Fireflies would be exploding, not lighting up.

Joseph waved the flashlight back and forth between the periodic table and the reaction on the easel. His thoughts bounced back and forth with it.

His mind wandered back to his journey.

Life had taken him many places and taught him many lessons. Joseph couldn't help but realize that the one thing he had learned was that the world was balanced; there was symmetry and perfection in everything. He thought about his experiences with poverty and riches. When he gave to the world, he received much. When he tried to take from the world, the world responded by taking back. He thought of the perfect balance of life. He reflected on the elements on the periodic table. The positive charges balanced the negative. Sleep balanced wakefulness. There was night and day. Male and female. Fear and freedom. Life and death.

Joseph wondered, *"If the world is so balanced, so perfect, so beautiful, why are the elements that give birth to all this life asymmetrical?"*

"That's it," he thought. *"That's what's missing. Symmetry. Balance."*

Joseph had it.

He looked again at the periodic table. He scanned through the columns and rows of elements searching for imbalance. He looked at his easel. He studied the firefly's reaction.

When he knew what he was finally looking for, it was obvious. There was imbalance in the periodic table, just as there was an imbalance in the reaction depicted on his easel. Balance was the key to unlock the mystery of the firefly's light.

In that moment everything changed. Suddenly, the periodic table took on a whole new shape.

It became clear — balanced — and far less complex than what he had been taught in school many years ago.

Mentally, Joseph spliced out the so-called "transition metals." It became clear to him that, just like Abram was able to find the sharps and flats of silicone, these transition metals were clearly the sharps and flats that laid beneath the balancing elements — germanium, tin, lead, and flerovium. All the so-called 4A elements were the perfectly mated pairs, the balancing elements.

Joseph liked his new definition of 4A elements as balancing elements.

The noble gases he renamed the birthing elements, just as Abram had explained when they were searching for the material for Joseph's sleep device. The noble gases were the "zero" elements that give birth to positive- and negative-charged mated pairs.

"How have people not recognized this before?" Joseph wondered in amazement.

He assumed it was because people were afraid to question the status quo. People just accepted what was, just as his colleagues had feared to question the dreaming problem of their patients.

Joseph looked at the second row of the periodic table.

Helium was the "zero" element, the noble gas, the birthing element, of the row above. Helium gave birth to positive- and negative-mated pairs. Lithium was the 1+ mate of florine 1-. Beryllium was the 2+ male of the 2- female oxygen. Boron was the electropositive 3+ counterpart of its mate, 3- nitrogen. Carbon was the center of united mates, the combined 4+/4-, male/female perfection. Carbon was the balancing element of the row. It was a perfect mixture of male and female, plus and minus.

Joseph scanned up just one row higher. He stared at hydrogen.

"That can't be right."

Joseph looked closer. He looked for balance.

"It's hydrogen!" Joseph exclaimed in revelation.

"If hydrogen is a 1+ element it must have a 1- mate. Plus, there must be a birthing element to give rise to the male hydrogen and its female counterpoint."   Knowledge was flowing through Joseph.

"There also should be other pairs, as well, to match the symmetry of the row below. There must be 2+/2- and 3+/3- elements.

"The periodic table is incomplete!

"To create symmetry and balance there has to be eight elements in each row. The hydrogen row is woefully incomplete."

Joseph looked back to his easel.

Just as the periodic table morphed in a flash, the reaction responsible for the firefly's light became clear. Its imbalance was obvious. It needed the 3- element from hydrogen's row to work.

Joseph decided to call this new element "kevion." He diagramed the new element on the easel and continued to talk himself through the mechanism.

"With kevion, the reaction works. It just needs an intermediate step with kevion.

"When kevion comes into contact with the high potential adenylate — the second, prior, missing step in the reaction — they combine to form not oxyluciferin, as was once believed, but rather keviluciferin!

"Keviluciferin relaxes from its excited state to emit light!"

Joseph had done it. He solved the mystery of the firefly. He knew how these beautiful creatures carried the light right inside of them. He unriddled that which had stumped the great scientific minds before him.

Joseph had discovered a new element — kevion — uncovering the essence of bioluminescence in the firefly.

He also had reason to believe there were several other elements that no one even knew existed.

"Oh, the possibilities," Joseph thought to himself.

"One step at a time." Joseph disciplined his thoughts, trying to focus and channel the ecstasy flowing through him.

If he could isolate kevion through the combination of the ingredients of luciferin, ATP and oxygen, then all he would have to do is mix kevion with a high-potential molecule and — voila — light! No electricity needed. No heat generated.

It hit Joseph.

"This could change the world...electricity-free light"

Joseph now had a new gift to give to the world; light to illumine the way.

‡

Joseph decided to walk the dark streets knowing shortly all paths would be lit, night and day. He stopped by the lake, dropped his feet in, and laid back. He breathed deeply.

"Are you ok?" a familiar voice asked.

Joseph turned his head, smiling at Abram.

"Wonderful."

Abram smiled back.

"So tell me, did you figure it out?"

"How did you know I was trying to figure something out?" Joseph asked with a wry smile.

"Last time we met, you told me something seemed to be missing on the periodic table. I figured you'd solved it by now," he responded with a grin.

Joseph looked back up at the sky and stars.

"The birthing element of hydrogen and its children," Joseph replied, with a sense the old man knew of them already.

Abram gave Joseph an impressed nod.

"The birthing element of hydrogen, huh?"

"Just like you said," Joseph explained, "the siblings have to come from somewhere. I thought 'parton' would be a good name for it."

"I like that very much," Abram said. "And the children, how did you find them?"

Motioning with a nod of the head, Joseph pointed to a firefly glowing.

"The light inside these little guys showed me the way."

"Smart little fellows aren't they?" Abram replied. "Luckily we carry the light in us as well."

Joseph shot a curious look at the old man.

"What do you mean?"

"I mean we have the light right inside us as well; most people just don't listen."

"We are supposed to listen to a light inside us?" Joseph asked, quite confused.

"I thought you knew. It's what you've always done in your lab."

Joseph widened his eyes waiting for him to continue.

"Yourdrum."

"Yourdrum?" Joseph repeated as he put his hand on his chest where his golden necklace used to hang from his neck, thinking of the beautiful woman who had been so elusive throughout his life.

"Joseph, you know yourdrum. Yourdrum is balance; it is silence. It's the guide within you, the map that leads you on your own path. It is the compass of the heart."

Joseph listened intently wanting Abram to continue, to give him more.

"When you listen to yourdrum, you hear silence. It's when you stray from yourdrum that it beats from the imbalance of wrong thinking and wrong action. Yourdrum tells you when you have gone astray from the desires of the heart, from following your true path."

Joseph nodded with comprehension, but still desired more.

"How do you know if you are following yourdrum?" Joseph asked.

"Perhaps an example from your life will help?" offered Abram.

Joseph nodded.

"When you moved into your lab, how did you feel? From the outside looking in, some would have thought your life was falling apart. But from the inside out, from your perspective, you had a deep, peaceful knowing, an unreasonable assuredness. When you follow yourdrum, this peaceful knowing is always with you."

It was true. When Joseph moved into his lab, he had an illogical assurance that he could create the device that would allow people to dream again. No one believed in it. No one believed in him. But he knew.

"And time can tell you as well," the old man continued.

"Time?"

"Oh, yes. Time is one of the clearest sign posts you're given. When you listen to yourdrum, time disappears, hours go by in seconds.

"Tell me, when you were developing your device, did not days run into weeks into months — timelessly?"

"That is true," Joseph admitted. "Seven months went by in the lab in the blink of an eye. It was by every measure uncomfortable — small and hot, no electricity, limited food. I was alone. But I was lost in creation."

"Exactly. In losing yourself, you found your true self, the self that can create masterpieces, creations that endure, gifts to give to the world. The inspiration of the creation re-inspires all who come in contact with it.

Everything the old man said rang with truth.

"Effort is the next way you can know if you're listening to yourdrum. By anyone's account, you were working impossible hours in rough conditions. Yet how did it feel?" Abram asked.

"That's right," Abram continued. "Work became effortless, much like time disappeared. You tapped into the endless supply of energy that rests within all, yet is tapped by few. This energy is not that which is provided by bread and water; it's the infinite energy of desire, supplied in proportion to the desire. Deep within, you had a desire to impact the world, to give to the world. This was the energy that powered you and made your work effortless.

"When you listen to yourdrum, you create the life you were meant to live, the life that is written deep within your heart. When you listen, it whispers the secrets to your every desire, the secrets to create masterpieces, to work effortlessly, to make time vanish.

"I don't understand. Why doesn't everyone listen to yourdrum?"

"I think you know the answer to that. Yourdrum is innate, demonstrated by the naturalness for children to fearlessly dream and believe. Yet, our culture is built to extinguish the very essence of life. We teach the importance of comfort and security; we preach reason and practicality. We admonish the naivety of dreamers and believers. We rebuke boldness and risk taking for stupidity. We ingrain fear instead of love into the hearts of our children.

"This fear creates the first imbalance in yourdrum. Yourdrum beats to lead those lost back to their path. The further one deviates, the louder yourdrum beats.

"You're then left with two options. The first is that you can choose fear. The second is that you can choose freedom. Unfortunately, we exalt the choice of fear in society.

Choosing fear drowns out yourdrum. Disguised as *"logic,"* *"reasoning,"* and *"practicality,"* fear is justified and lauded in society.

"Nearly everyone at some point in their life gets trapped in the decision between fear and freedom. They oscillate. Some days they can hear the beat, other days they hear doubt more loudly. Doubt is fear's tool to rob us of freedom.

"Yet, yourdrum does not give up easily. It continues to make itself known through symptoms such as sadness and depression, fatigue and lethargy, anxiety and restlessness. It tries to push you back on your path, to listen within, and forget what you hear without. But, we drown out these warnings with medications, with drugs, with distractions. Eventually, we become numb to the sound of the beat of yourdrum. Unless we have the courage to unbury it, peel away fear, and set aside doubt, yourdrum is muffled into the background, unable to provide the service of the heart for which it was created."

Joseph listened intently.

"Most people have created a life designed to keep your-drum at bay — a life built around supposed security and comfort, a life built around distractions, a life confined to the walls of their comfort zones.

"You can live a life of struggle, of quiet desperation, a life of constant tension and effort, fighting to live in the comfort of the walls you have built for yourself — walls that provide a false sense of safety and security. You can continue to wrap a blanket around your heart and smoth-er the beat of yourdrum. You can choose to listen to the noises that shake your senses rather than the silence of your all-powerful, all-knowing drum.

"Or you can live a life of freedom by tearing these walls down. As you know, stepping outside the house you've built for comfort is scary. But it is the way to liberation. It is freedom.

"Once you step outside, once you turn up the volume, then you can hear it again. Then the beat becomes clear. You can see your dreams. Hearing yourdrum means you have conquered fear to the extent that you can hear it. But hearing yourdrum is not the ultimate goal. Listening to it is where your life lies."

"So there is a difference between hearing yourdrum and listening to it?" Joseph asked.

"Most assuredly," the old man continued. "Hearing yourdrum is directing you where to go, listening to it is going there."

"Can you elaborate on this?" Joseph asked, wanting to be sure he understood.

"The beating of yourdrum comes with two beats. The first beat is to inform you when you are straying from your balance, your heart's desires, your true path. This beat is trying to force you onto the right path. Yourdrum uses its beat to create discomfort, uneasiness, restlessness, and a sense of confinement to try and move you back to your path. Yourdrum does whatever it can so that you can hear it.

"The other beat balances the first. It is the beat of ecstasy. This beat comes as intuition, revelation, eureka moments of epiphany. When you embrace and live in ecstasy, you are listening to yourdrum. Yourdrum's beats are man's aid to living his life, his desires, his destiny. It's how man fulfills his dreams. Once you hear yourdrum, you can listen to it; and when you listen, you live in the peace of ecstasy. Your creations are from your true self; they are perfect, and they endure. They give love, which is as surely to return as night follows day."

"You mean we are predestined on a certain path?" Joseph asked, seeking full knowledge and understanding.

"Yes and no. There is that which makes you *Joseph*. It's not the language you speak or the color of your skin, but the Joseph behind the mask. This Joseph was born with unique desires, intrinsic passions. And this Joseph was given the ability to fulfill all of his desires and live a full, majestic life — one that is a gift to the rest of the world. Of course, you are given the choice to live this life of blissful ecstasy and the choice to live otherwise."

Joseph understood.

"It appears that most people only hear with their eardrums and put all their faith in their senses in order to reason and justify. But this is done at the expense of being able to hear yourdrum."

Abram smiled as a master would who succeeded in passing down his knowledge to his disciple.

‡

Joseph knew the ingredients. Now he just needed the tools to create the bioluminescence of the firefly's light. Luckily, he knew a place — the SCI.

Prying open a side window, Joseph squeezed himself head first into the SCI. Once inside, Joseph knew what his first step must be — confirm his discovery of kevion.

"How do you see something you can't see?" Joseph thought.

He knew the answer.

"Light of course. Look at the light spectrum."

Joseph uncovered the spectrometer. If kevion exists, he should be able to see its wavelength in the spectrum of helium.

With a smile of victory as he looked through the spectrometer, Joseph saw it. A wavelength of 492 nanometers confirmed the existence of kevion, validating the possibility of light without electricity or heat.

Just as Joseph confirmed his discovery of kevion, he heard a knock and the sound of a key unlocking the main door.

"Hello?" It was the voice of the rugged man.

Joseph turned towards the door, not at all concerned that he was trespassing.

"You weren't gone long," the rugged man said, recognizing Joseph. "What brings you back so soon?"

"Ah," Joseph thought, trying to find an explanation that didn't seem completely insane. "I think I discovered something," he vaguely answered.

"Discovered something?"

"Yes…"

"You mean to tell me after all the time and work in the SCI with the smartest minds in the world, you could produce nothing; but you return home and make a discovery overnight?"

Joseph nodded with a sheepish grin.

"Well, do tell me about this discovery...," the rugged man pressed, crossing his arms over his chest and leaning against the doorframe.

"Fireflies. I've always wondered how they worked, how they managed to carry light right inside their bodies. It never made sense to me. Scientifically, it didn't make sense. Scientists assumed the light came from a reaction that just shouldn't work."

"Really?" The rugged man walked over to Joseph, taking a seat next to the spectrometer.

"Last night, I went about trying to uncover this mystery. I think I stumbled upon some elements that we never knew existed. One of these elements, I believe, is responsible for the firefly's bioluminescence."

"Is that right? How does one go about stumbling upon new elements exactly?" the rugged man asked in delighted puzzlement. "I imagine these elements weren't just sitting on your doorstep."

"Not exactly. These particular elements can't be seen with the human eye. They're gases in ambient conditions."

"So you discovered new gases. How did you manage that?"

"Well, I thought about the reaction that most scientists believe happens inside the firefly and how it didn't make sense. Just accepting it had always been unsettling to me. Something was clearly missing in the reaction. Then it hit me. I had the same thought about the periodic table. Something had always seemed missing.

"I thought back to life and how it's always so perfectly balanced; yet this reaction and the elements of the periodic table are not. Once I had this clarity, it was obvious. The reaction was unbalanced just like the periodic table was unbalanced. In a flash, I saw the periodic table in a completely new light. I saw new elements and their rightful places."

"Undiscovered elements?" The rugged man was fascinated. Joseph knew if he told this to anyone else he would be admonished as a heretic.

"I believe so. See, hydrogen has a 1+ charge, but no one had ever asked where its 1- mate is, or realized that it had to have a mate. Moreover, no one had asked where the element is that gives rise to the 1+ hydrogen. No one had ever realized that these element pairs had to arise from a birthing element."

"A birthing element?" the rugged man repeated with a curious tone.

"Yes...the noble gases, the elements that don't react or join with any other elements, these are birthing elements. I believe they give rise to the mated pairs: 1+/1-, 2+/2-, 3+/3-, and 4+/-. The 4+/- is a mated union, like carbon and silicone. These 4A elements are balancing elements. They are symmetrical perfection. It just so happens that kevion, I believe, is an element offspring of an unknown noble gas, a birthing element yet to be discovered. Kevion should have a 3- charge and a chemical structure that makes the firefly's internal chemical reaction work."

"Kevion?" The rugged man was dumbfounded, capable of only single-word responses.

"Kevion. That's what I named the element. Do you have something better in mind?"

The rugged man laughed in amazement. "No, kevion sounds great. So what's next?"

"Well, that's why I'm here. First, I needed to confirm kevion exists," Joseph explained. "And so I used this spectrometer to look at helium's line spectrum," he said as he put his hand on the instrument.

The rugged man looked over at the spectrometer next to him.

"You see, you can use these expensive tools to see some pretty incredible things, like spectra of wavelengths. I guess the SCI wasn't a complete waste after all," Joseph smirked.

"Now we just need to gather some of the molecules in the reaction and isolate kevion before it reacts with the intermediate in the second step of the reaction. Then we will have light potential in a bottle!"

"Is this difficult to do?"

"Well, thankfully, I squandered my past fortune on the SCI. Its expensive instruments allow us to do this quite simply. In a couple days or so, I'll have kevion ready to light the world."

The rugged man paused for a second in thought.

"Joseph, I think there's someone I would like you to meet."

‡

Joseph worked nonstop the next four days isolating kevion, testing, and creating bioluminescence on command. A knock on the door of the SCI interrupted his tireless concentration.

"Mind if I come in?" the rugged man asked, carrying a plate of food. "I figured you needed to eat. If you die, your discovery may never see the light of day."

Joseph smiled at his new friend's wit.

"I said I had someone I'd like you to meet. If you have a minute, I'd like to introduce you."

"Of course," Joseph said.

"Tom, come on in," the rugged man called. "Tom, this is Joseph; Joseph, this is Tom, my boss."

No introduction was necessary.

The man who encouraged Joseph years ago to create his sleep device, the man who had an energy and enthusiasm unmatched by anyone Joseph had ever known, stood before him.

"Hi, Doc!" Tom exclaimed, surprised to see his old doctor.

"Tom! Great to see you!" Joseph said with incredulous shock, as he started to connect the dots.

Tom was the rugged man's boss, the one who owned one of the largest businesses in the world, and widely considered the wealthiest man alive. He was the inventor who controlled and operated the majority of the electricity in the world.

"You two know each other?" the rugged man asked, as surprised as Joseph and Tom were to see each other.

Tom put his hand on the rugged man's shoulder.

"Our friend told me about your discovery, Doc," Tom explained. "But he didn't tell me it was by the famous Dr. Joseph!"

The rugged man laughed.

"I had no idea he was your doctor."

"Well, Doc, you have quite the knack for discovery!" Tom laughed.

"Thank you, Tom. I wouldn't be here if it weren't for you and your encouragement." Joseph replied.

"You had a great theory and a great idea to solve a big dreaming problem. I couldn't let you just give up on it — for your sake and the world's sake.

"I think our friend here told you, I have a business that provides electricity to a good portion of the world. I wanted to let you know that I'm happy and eager to help you get your discovery into the households of the world. If what I've heard is true, we could light the world on a fraction of a percent of the energy we currently use. And I think that's wonderful."

Joseph nodded and showed Tom his calculations.

"If my estimates are correct, it should be about .004 percent of the energy required of our soon-to-be-extinct tungsten filament."

Joseph then demonstrated kevion and electricity-free light. Tom lit up with excitement.

Joseph noted that instead of being threatened by the possibility of kevion wrecking his empire, Tom was thrilled. He was as excited as if he himself had made the discovery. Joseph remembered the rugged man's story about how this inventor tried to help his competitors after he had discovered how to produce electricity with half the waste at half the costs. Tom truly was selfless in his giving to the world.

The three men sat and discussed the implications of kevion.

The global impact of the discovery was incalculable. Those who lived in the dark would now have a limitless supply of light. The energy saved would start to reverse the damage done by the burning of fossil fuels. Pollutants would be kept out of the atmosphere, creating a brighter, healthier world.

Joseph and Tom worked for several days formulating a plan that would use Tom's business infrastructure to produce and distribute kevion at scale. With their partnership solidified, Joseph and Tom set out to bring a new light into the world.

‡

Eight months later, Joseph received a letter from Sweden. It was addressed to "Dr. Joseph," but mailed to the SCI, which the rugged man still owned. Joseph was sure it was misaddressed. He assumed that it must be for his rugged, traveler friend, as he had never been to Sweden. Joseph walked out of the SCI where he had spent much time with Tom over the last year. He found the rugged man tending his crops.

"I have something for you," Joseph shouted as he approached.

"Hi, Joseph, how is everything progressing?"

"Wonderfully," Joseph responded. "We expanded into two more countries this week."

"So you're still on pace for world domination?" the rugged man joked.

Joseph laughed.

"I have a letter for you. Well, it's addressed to me; but it's from Sweden, so I assume it's a mistake and it's for you," Joseph explained. "How is Sweden by the way?"

"Sweden? In all my travels, I've never been there. Need to add it to my bucket list," he replied.

"Hm…" Joseph muttered curiously.

Joseph opened the letter and read aloud.

> *Doctor Joseph,*
>
> *We hope this finds you well. We are writing to inform you that you have been selected as a Laureate for the Nobel Prize in Chemistry. Your discovery of kevion and its application to provide heatless, electricity-free light is of the highest accomplishment. We are requesting your acceptance to be recognized as a Nobel Prize Laureate and the accompanying monetary award and golden*

medal. This is but a small token of gratitude for the world's indebtedness to you. Upon your acceptance, we request your presence December 10 at the Stockholm Concert Hall and the Nobel Banquet so we may publicly display our gratitude and bestow you with the honor you so justly deserve.

Thank you,

Nobel Committee

Royal Swedish Academy of Sciences

The rugged man beamed at Joseph.

"I hope you know I'm coming along with you," he said with a smile. "I have to cross Sweden off my bucket list."

Joseph stood silent for a moment.

"Nobel Laureate." Joseph was stunned. This was a dream beyond his dream. A dream he didn't know if he was ready for yet.

"But we still have so much work to do…" Joseph said half to the rugged man, half to himself, as he started back towards the SCI in a daze.

Joseph had changed. He was concerned only with what he could give to the world. Rewards and recognition lost all importance; fame and fortune were the last things on his mind.

‡

Eight weeks later, in early December, the rugged man came into the SCI to pry Joseph away from his work.

"We're going," he said.

Joseph continued studying the graphs on his desk in front of him.

"I will use force if necessary," the rugged man continued with a smile.

Joseph turned and looked at his friend.

"They aren't expecting me."

"They are expecting you."

"What do you mean?"

"I confirmed your acceptance for you," the rugged man said.

Joseph's eyes widened.

"And don't give me that look," the rugged man continued. "The letter was sent to my address. And, remember, you're still working in *my* lab," he said with a grin.

Joseph's head collapsed against his chest, reluctantly giving in to his friend's persistence. They were off to Sweden.

‡

Joseph stood behind the stage at the Stockholm Concert Hall, receiving instructions on how he should enter and accept his award. His companion on the journey to Sweden, the rugged man, had a seat out in the audience. Tom was also meeting them there for the celebration. Joseph peeked out from behind the stage, but he couldn't see his friends among the massive crowd.

"It's with great pleasure I introduce the next presenter," the King of Sweden announced from the podium. "He will grant the award to the Nobel Laureate in Chemistry. Please welcome to the stage, Nobel Laureate himself, the renowned scientist, Dr. Abram Hamilton!"

The crowd erupted in applause.

Dr. Hamilton made his way up the stairs and to the podium.

"Thank you, thank you." Dr. Hamilton waved his hand. "It is an honor to be here with you this evening and a special honor to present the award to our latest Laureate in Chemistry."

The woman giving Joseph instructions backstage put her hand on his back, telling Joseph to get ready. The presenter's voice sounded familiar to Joseph. The woman distracting him with instructions, and the rumble of the crowd prevented him from being able to place it, though.

"This young man did what all great scientists do," Dr. Hamilton continued. "He questioned assumptions. He looked within himself for answers. He dared to dream. And he was bold enough to believe in himself."

The crowd erupted in applause again.

"Please join me in honoring the man who discovered the element kevion, the man who is bringing a new light into all of our lives, Dr. Joseph!"

At the call of his name, Joseph exited from behind the stage and made his way up the stairs, deafened by the roar of the audience. As he stepped up onto the platform, he froze.

"Abram."

He couldn't believe his eyes. The strange old man from the lake was a renowned scientist, a beacon in the field of chemistry.

As Joseph continued toward the podium, Abram shot him a wink and a grin.

"Congratulations, Dr. Joseph," Abram said as they shook hands, and he handed Joseph the golden medal.

Joseph was speechless. He turned to the King of Sweden and shook hands. The King bestowed Joseph with his Nobel Laureate diploma. With his medal and diploma in hand, the most prestigious award and symbol of scientific achievement in the world, Joseph looked out at the packed concert hall. His hearing was muted. Silence permeated his head. He watched as the crowd stood and clapped, but the standing ovation was inaudible.

Joseph smiled and acknowledged the audience, bowing in gratitude.

Abram put his arm around Joseph, ushered him off the stage and over to the Blue Hall where the celebration continued at the Nobel Banquet.

Bursting with over a thousand guests, the Blue Hall awaited Joseph's arrival. He entered to more cheering and applause. A pipe organ filled the hall with jubilant music. As the Swedish royal family greeted Joseph at the door, his attention was transfixed to the balcony.

There she was.

Her bright blue eyes caught his. Standing at the edge of the balcony above, she smiled down at Joseph. Her beauty was even more pronounced than he remembered; it contrasted with the rugged appearance of the man who stood next to her.

Excusing himself from the royal family, Joseph made his way up the spiral staircase. Abram followed close behind. Wading through the crowd, Joseph and Abram made it to the balcony.

Her beautiful blue eyes, long dark hair, and gentle smile took Joseph's breath away.

"Hello." She smiled.

"Hi," Joseph said with a clash of excitement and confusion. "How…?"

The beautiful woman walked around behind Joseph. She put her arms around his neck and fastened the golden drum around him.

"Would you like to explain?" she nodded at the rugged man.

Joseph clutched the golden drum against his chest.

"We can explain together," the rugged man replied.

"Joseph when we first met, you were wearing that necklace. I recognized it, but couldn't remember where I'd seen it. I took it as a good omen though, and it's why I sold my land to you," the rugged man explained.

"When you fell on hard times and offered it to me as payment, my curiosity got the best of me; and I accepted the bribe. A few weeks later, after you'd lost your castle, and I found you on the street, it reminded me of the times I had no possessions. I was moved to tell you my story. In relating my travels, I thought back to my time in Italy where I briefly made friends with a musician. He was a famous drummer who travelled the world playing for large audiences. During his stop in Italy, he stayed in my home; and we spent much of the week together talking about the world, our travels, and our next adventures.

"That night, talking to you on the street, it struck me that he wore the same necklace. I hadn't heard from him in years, but I tracked Ethan down and brought him the necklace. Ethan told me it wasn't his anymore. But this beautiful young lady said she knew who it belonged to."

"I held on to the necklace, waiting for the right time to deliver it to its rightful owner," the beautiful woman explained. "When you returned to your lab, it was clear you were back on the right path. I've been waiting anxiously since to return yourdrum."

"Thank you," Joseph said, overflowing with love and gratitude. He put his arms around the beautiful woman. The rugged man put a hand on his shoulder. Tom smiled on.

Abram watched as a proud father would on his son's happiest day.

The five looked at each other, sharing in the moment of love.

"Shall we go celebrate downstairs?" the rugged man asked.

Tom nodded in agreement, but Joseph and Abram weren't thinking about the party.

Abram looked at Joseph, reading his mind.

"What about that other element? That birthing element — what did you call it?" Abram asked.

"Parton," Joseph replied, more to himself than to Abram.

"Parton?" Tom repeated curiously.

"Yes," Joseph responded with a smile. "The undiscovered, birthing element of hydrogen and kevion…"

Abram winked knowingly at Joseph.

Yourdrum was loud and clear.

Out of the corner of his eye, Joseph saw the beautiful, long, dark hair waving as it flowed down the staircase. Joseph knew where he was headed — back to his lab.

YOURDRUM

Travels of Yourdrum continued...

Travels of Yourdrum

"sadly, most books sit on shelves"

Name:

From (where you purchased/received/found it):

_____

_____

Passed Along (where you gifted/dropped/sent it):

_____

_____

_____

Name: _____

From (where you purchased/received/found it):

_____

_____

Passed Along (where you gifted/dropped/sent it):

_____

_____

_____

TRAVELS OF YOURDRUM

"it's often hard to tell if you found the book or if it found you"

Name: _____

From (where you purchased/received/found it):

_____

_____

Passed Along (where you gifted/dropped/sent it):

_____

_____

_____

Name: _____

From (where you purchased/received/found it):

_____

_____

Passed Along (where you gifted/dropped/sent it):

_____

_____

_____

Travels of Yourdrum

"giving and receiving are two sides of the same coin"

Name: _____

From (where you purchased/received/found it):

_____

_____

Passed Along (where you gifted/dropped/sent it):

_____

_____

_____

Name: _____

From (where you purchased/received/found it):

_____

_____

Passed Along (where you gifted/dropped/sent it):

_____

_____

_____

TRAVELS OF YOURDRUM

"a book worth reading is one without an ending"

Name: _____

From (where you purchased/received/found it):

_____

_____

Passed Along (where you gifted/dropped/sent it):

_____

_____

_____

Name: _____

From (where you purchased/received/found it):

_____

_____

Passed Along (where you gifted/dropped/sent it):

_____

_____

_____